THE TORY MAID

Please see www.wildsidepress.com for a complete list!

THE TORY MAID

HERBERT BAIRD STIMPSON

WILDSIDE PRESS

THE TORY MAID

To
Rev. Dr. and Mrs. Hall Harrison
this volume
is affectionately inscribed by
the Author

CHAPTER I

WE START FOR THE WAR

I, James Frisby of Fairlee, in the county of Kent, on the eastern shore of what was known in my youth as the fair Province of Maryland, but now the proud State of that name, growing old in years, but hearty and hale withal, though the blood courses not through my veins as in the days of my youth, sit on the great porch of Fairlee watching the sails on the distant bay, where its gleaming waters meet the mouth of the creek that runs at the foot of Fairlee. A julep there is on the table beside me, flavoured with mint gathered by the hands of John Cotton early in the morning, while the dew was still upon it, from the finest bank in all Kent County.

So with these old friends around me, with the julep on my right hand and the paper before me, I sit on the great porch of Fairlee to write of the wild days of my youth, when I first drew my sword in the Great Cause. To write, before my hand becomes feeble and my eyes grow dim, of the strange things that I saw and the adventures that befell me, of the old Tory of the Braes, of the fair maid his daughter, and of the part they played in my life during the War of the Deliverance. To write so that those who come after me, as well as those who are growing up around my knees, may know the part their grandfather played in the stirring times that proclaimed the birth of a mighty nation.

The first year of the great struggle, ah, me! I was young then, and the wild blood was in my veins. I was broad of shoulder and long of limb, with a hand that gripped like steel and a seat in the saddle that was the envy of all that hard-riding country. I was hardy and skilled in all the outdoor sports and pastimes of my race and people, and being light in the saddle I often led the hardest riders and won from them the brush, while every creek for fifty miles up and down the broad Chesapeake, and even the farther shore as far as Baltimore, knew my canoe, and the High Sheriff himself was no finer shot than I.

You, who bask in the sunshine of long and dreary years of peace, who never hear the note of the bugle nor see the flash of the foeman's steel from one year's end to another, know not what it was to live in those stirring times and all the joy of the strife. You should have seen us then, when the whole land was aflame.

The fiery signal had come like a rush of the wind from the north, with the cry of the dying on the roadsides and fields of

Lexington.

All along the western shore the men of Anne Arundel, of Frederick, and Prince George were mustering fast and strong. Then the Kentish men and those of Queen Anne and all the lower shore were mounting fast and mustering, while from the Howard hills came riding down bold and hardy yeomen.

Then, and as it has always been in the old province of Maryland, the gentlemen led the people, and everywhere the spirit of fire ran like molten steel through the veins of the gathering hosts, and the people took up the gauntlet of war with a laugh and a cheer and shook their clenched hands at the King who was over the sea; so it was the length and breadth of the province, and so it was with me.

And so one day the signal came, and I mounted my black colt Toby and rode away to the Head of Elk in the county of Cecil, where the mustering was, to take my place, as it was my duty and right to do, side by side with the bravest gentlemen of the province in the coming struggle for the Great Cause.

I was eighteen in the month of March of that year and considered myself a man, and, having reached man's estate, I bade good-bye to my mother and rode from out the sheltering walls and groves of Fairlee.

But just before I rode within the shadow of the great woods I turned in my saddle and waved my hand to the small, quaint figure that stood on the broad porch watching me disappear; and she bravely—for the women were brave in those days—waved her hand in return, and then I rode on, for the moment saddened at the parting, for the die that day would be cast, and, though there would be mustering and drilling for many weeks before we took up our march to the northward, the hand of the cause would claim me as its own.

I was riding thus through the forest when I heard hoof-beats behind me and a cheery halloo, and who should ride up but Dick Ringgold of Hunting Field, a lad of my own age and my true friend?

"Why such a long face?" he laughed. "You look as if you were going to a funeral and not to a hunt that will beat all the runs to the hounds in the world. We are going to hunt redcoats and fair ladies' smiles and not foxes now; so cheer up, man."

"Plague on it, Dick, you are ten miles from home and I am only one," I retorted. "You ought to have seen how bravely her ladyship tried to smile, too."

"We will increase the number of miles then," said he, and

reaching over he struck Toby across the flank. Well, Toby needs the curb at best, and it was a full half-mile before I brought him up and had a chance to give Dick a rating.

But Dick only laughed.

And so we rode on, across the low-lying plains of Kent, northward toward the borders of Cecil.

For miles we would ride under the shadow of the dense forest, and then we would come to the wide-reaching fields of some great manor or plantation, the manor house itself generally crowning some gently rising knoll amid a grove of trees, with a view of the distant bay, or creek, or river, as the case might be; the cluster of houses, the quarters for the slaves, the stables and the barns, making little villages and hamlets amid the wide expanse of farm lands and the distant circle of the dark green forests.

Then, again, a creek or river would bar our course, and we would have to ride for miles until we turned its head, or found a ferry or a ford, and so overcome its opposition. So on we rode until, as the day waxed near the noon hour, we came to the little hamlet of Georgetown, nestling amid the hills on the banks of the Sassafras. Crossing the river at the ferry, we began the last stage of our journey.

The trail now skirted the broad lands of Bohemia Manor, and crossed the beautiful river of that name, embedded between the hills and wide-stretching farm lands.

As we approached the banks of the Elk the country grew more rolling and wilder—in our front the Iron Hills rose up before us, crowned with forests, in sharp contrast to the low-lying country through which we had been passing.

And now, as our appetites became pressing, we urged our horses on, for we had still many miles to travel.

CHAPTER II

WE MEET THE MAID

We had just come in sight of the blue waters of the Elk, as it rolled between the forest-clad hills on either side, basking here for a moment in the sunshine, then lost in the deeper shadows of the overhanging forest.

"There rolls the Elk," cried Dick. "Only ten miles more, and a stroke upon a piece of paper, and then, my boy, you are done for. A pain that eats its way ever inward, a thirst that never slackens, and over all the black night lowering down. Aye, so it is, Sir Monk of the Long Face; but we will have some fun before we are put under the sod or our bones are left to whiten on the sands."

"That we will, Sir Richard. And now we are in for it, for here comes our first adventure. Is she ugly or is she fair? Which, Sir Richard?"

For, as we reached the point where our road joins the river road, we saw, approaching along the lower road, a gentleman riding on a powerful horse, while behind him on a pillion sat a slight girlish figure, hidden in part by the broad shoulders of the rider.

"By Jove, it is Gordon of the Braes," said Dick.

"What, the suspected Tory?"

"Yes; and that must be his daughter. They say she is the fairest lass in all the county of Cecil."

"Tory or no Tory," said I, "with a fair face at stake, I will speak to him."

They were as yet some distance off, but as the rider drew nearer to us we saw that he was a splendid specimen of manhood, such as I had but seldom seen before.

While strong of frame and above the medium height, he carried himself and rode with a courtliness and ease that bespoke the accomplished horseman and gentleman. His splendid head and face showed the marks of an adventurous career, and all bespoke the blood of the family from which he had sprung, the Gordons of Avochie.

But striking as was the figure of the rider, the glimpse we caught of the fair burden behind made us for the moment forget him.

A slender figure it was that sat upon the pillion, with wonderful eyes of the darkest blue and hair of the deepest brown that waved and clustered around the temples—a mouth that was winsome and sweet, a small and aristocratic nose, a chin that was slightly determined, giving her altogether a queenly air, as she sat so straight and prim behind her father.

"Sir," said I, making Toby advance and bowing to his mane, "as we are travelling the same way, will you permit us to accompany you? My friend is Richard Ringgold of Hunting Field and I am James Frisby of Fairlee."

"It will give me pleasure," he replied, saluting courteously, "to have your company to the Head of Elk. I know your families and your houses well, and you, no doubt, have heard of me, Charles Gordon of the Braes."

"That we have," said Dick Ringgold. "It was only a week ago that my mother spoke of your first coming to old Kent."

"It was kind of her to remember me," he replied. "She was a great belle and a beauty in her youth."

Dick smiled with pleasure, and I, taking advantage of a narrow place in the road, fell behind, and rode so I could talk to Mistress Jean, much to Master Richard's secret indignation. But she received me with a show of displeasure, and though I courteously asked her of her journey, it was some minutes before I knew the cause thereof.

"Are you not," said she, and her aristocratic little head was in the air, "afraid to be seen riding with suspected Tories, you who wear the black cockade?"

And then I remembered that I wore the emblem of our party.

"Afraid!" I replied. "Afraid! We who have bearded the Ministers of the Crown in the broad light of day? Do you think I am afraid of our own men? Why, if Mistress North herself were half as fair as your ladyship of the Braes, I would ride with her through all the armies of the patriots, and no man would dare say me nay."

A merry twinkle came into her eyes. "Would you wear the red cockade if she should ask you?"

"Ah, Mistress Jean, would you seduce me from my allegiance to the cause of the patriots?"

"To the cause of the patriots? What of your allegiance to the King?"

"But the King himself has broken that, and forced us in self-defence to take up arms in revolt. Would you have me true to my people, or to the King, who is over the sea?"

"To the King," she answered promptly, "for the King's Ministers may be bad men today and good tomorrow, but if you once strike a blow at the mother country and win, then the ties of love, of friendship, and of interest are severed for ever."

"Yes; but she should have thought of that before she forced us to it."

"What spoiled children you are," she cried. "Because the taffy is not as good as usual you want to pull the house down about our ears."

Thus receiving and parrying thrusts, we rode along the banks of the Elk, and as we neared the ferry we met numbers of men travelling the same way with us, all bound for the great mustering, and though they returned our salutations, seeing the black cockade in our hats, they scowled on Gordon of the Braes.

"There goes that dog of a Tory," I would hear them growl to one another as we passed.

But Gordon rode on with a cool, indifferent, almost contemptuous manner, which made the frowns grow blacker, and the mutterings deeper and louder. But no man as yet sought to beard him, for his courage and his daring were well known throughout the shore, and it would have taken a bold man indeed to cross Gordon of the Braes.

At last we came to the ferry and saw on the hillside, among the forest trees, the white tents, already taking on the appearance of a well-regulated camp. The little town amid the trees, busy with the life of the moving crowd, and bright with the uniforms of the Maryland Line, which we were soon to don, formed a curious spectacle as we entered.

Every part of the province was represented. Here was a tall backwoodsman in his coonskin cap, buckskin shirt and leggings, with his long and deadly rifle, totally unadorned by the glint of silver or chasing on the barrel to betray him to his redskin neighbour—and you knew that one of Cresap's riflemen was before you.

By his side, for the moment, was a young tobacco planter from Prince George. The youngster to whom he was talking, clad in the scarlet and buff of the Maryland Line, was a young dandy from Annapolis.

And so it was all through the crowd, the frontiersman, the hard-riding country squire, and the city swell, all mingled together, and all animated with one all-pervading and all-engrossing thought—how best to secure the freedom of the country and resist the tyranny of the King.

As we made our way through the crowd the faces grew dark as they saw the Tory, but as Dick and I rode on either hand, with our black cockades, the crowd murmuringly gave way before us, and though all the people were hostile to him, and he could not help but see it, he coolly looked them over and rode as if he had no enemy within a hundred miles.

But the colour in Mistress Jean's cheek flamed high, and I saw her little hands clenched together, as if she would like to tell these rebels what she thought of their treatment of her father. And I, seeing the war signal so clearly on her cheek, and daring not the batteries of her eyes and wit, was discreet and said not a word.

We took our way to the inn, kept by one John McLean, a genial host and Scotchman, who was well known in three provinces, and kept the finest inn for many miles around.

He received us in a jovial way, for though he was a stanch patriot, he and Gordon had been friends for many years.

"So, Mistress Jean, you have deigned to honour my roof with your presence. Welcome, welcome, all of you."

And though I had swung myself off Toby to assist Mistress Jean to dismount, he was before me and swung her lightly to the ground.

"I declare," he said, "you grow bonnier every day, lassie," which brought a blush to her cheek. Then, turning, he called his wife and placed Mistress Jean in her charge.

"I am sorry to say, gentlemen, that the inn is very crowded, as you see, but I think I can find a place for you." Then drawing the Tory aside for a little way, we heard him remonstrating with him for coming to the town at such a time, when the feeling ran so strong and high against the Loyalist.

"You risk your life," he said, "for the slightest spark or indiscretion will bring a mob, boiling and seething around you. The officers will not be able to hold the men in, as they are only volunteers, and have not yet felt the hand of discipline."

But Charles Gordon shrugged his shoulders, and his reply came distinct and clear: "I thought you knew me better, McLean. I would not hide my head for a hundred or a thousand of them;" and he turned and went into the inn.

The innkeeper made a gesture of despair. "That is always the way," said he, "both in this country and the old; tell a Gordon of a danger and he will rush right into it, and then expect to come out safe and sound."

We laughed, for the expression on the old Scotchman's face was so droll.

"But now for your room, gentlemen;" and he led the way to a small room under the gable roof. "It is the only room I have left," he said, "but you are welcome to it."

It was now somewhat late in the afternoon, but having made ourselves presentable and partaken of a lunch, we went to report ourselves to Captain Ramsay of the 1st Regiment of the Maryland Line.

He received us at his tent door with a warm grasp of the hand. "You are the very lads I have been waiting for," he said. "I have two Lieutenancies to fill, and you are the men to fill them."

"But, Captain," said Dick Ringgold, "we have not been tried yet. Let us go into the ranks and fight our way up, as so many better men than we are doing."

I could not help admiring Dick for his modesty, and though I, too, said the same thing, I confess I hoped the Captain would not hear of it, and so it proved.

"No, no," he said, and patted Dick on the shoulder. "I must have you; I know the blood that runs in your veins, lads, and that I will have no better fighting stock in the army." And thus it was settled, and we became officers in that Maryland Line, and—I say it with all due modesty—the most famous of all the fighting regiments in the struggle for the Great Cause.

CHAPTER III

A FLASH OF STEEL

That night we sat at the long table in the dining-room of the inn. All up and down its great length sat the officers of the Line—country gentlemen from Cecil, Kent, and as far south as Queen Anne, who had ridden thus far to see the mustering and to give it their countenance and their favour. Grave and sedate gentlemen many of them, men of affairs, the leaders of their counties, and delegates to the Convention and to Congress—men of the oldest and bluest blood in the province, of wide estates and famous names, whose families wielded a mighty influence in the cause of the patriots and gave it stability and great strength.

Then there was the parson, a merry old gentleman, stout of form, with a round face and twinkling eyes, who in his youth was a mighty fox-hunter in spite of his cloth; even then, stout as he had grown, when he heard the music of the hounds, it was with difficulty he restrained the inclination to follow, which now, alas! was made impossible by his great weight. We who loved hard riding, hard fighting, and a strong will, admired him, and no man was more popular throughout the three counties than the fox-hunting parson. He knew the people and their ways, and was one of them.

"I hear you are fire-eaters here," he said to a vestryman upon being installed.

"Then we are well matched," came the reply, "for they say you are a pepperbox."

So no gathering throughout the county was a success without the parson, and by the unanimous voice of the Line he was called to be their chaplain.

We sat there in the long dining-room amid the hum of many voices, the glare of many lights, and the click of the glasses, as the wine was going around, when a young man who sat across the table from me rose with his glass poised between his fingers.

He was a handsome man, of twenty-one or twenty-two, of dark and swarthy features, thick lips and nose, and hair as black as night, telling of the Indian blood in his veins.

His name was Rodolph, and he was the son of a man more noted for his wealth than for his principles, but who was then at the city of Annapolis, a delegate from the county of Cecil.

"I propose a toast," he cried, "that all true patriots should drink. A toast to the delegates of this county, who at the convention of the province in the city of Annapolis are standing as the bulwarks of liberty against the tyranny of the Crown."

We were all on our feet in an instant to drink the toast, with a right goodwill, all except Charles Gordon, who sat at my right hand. He kept his seat and watched us with a cool, sarcastic smile upon his lips.

"Is not the toast good enough for you?" cried Rodolph, with an ugly sneer upon his face.

All eyes now turned to where Charles Gordon sat, and he slowly rose.

"Drink to your delegates?" said he. "Not I. They are the scum of the county of Cecil, and you know it. I would as soon be governed by my slaves at the Braes as by such men as they are. I wish you joy of them." And bowing, he turned and left the room by a door that was near at hand.

For an instant there was silence, then an uproar broke forth, and Rodolph sprang around the table to follow him, with several of the young men at his heels. But I, seeing the danger, with possibly a thought of a fair maid's eyes, threw myself before the door with drawn sword.

"No man passes through this door," I cried, "unless he passes over me."

The crowd drew back in surprise.

"Since when," I shouted, for they hesitated, "have Maryland gentlemen learned to fight in mobs? If any one has an insult to resent, let him fight as becomes a gentleman, man to man."

"Stand aside," shouted Rodolph, who was now before me, "and let me get at the traitor."

"Put up your swords, gentlemen." I found I had a new ally in a tall, dignified gentleman, who took his place beside me, a Mr. Wilmer of the White House in Kent.

"The lad is right," he said; "and you, Rodolph, I should think, would have had enough of Charles Gordon of the Braes."

At this there was a laugh, which at the time I did not understand; but the company good-naturedly put back their swords and resumed their places at the table, all except Rodolph, who slipped away from the room.

That night, as I lay upon my bed, dreaming, boylike, of the fair eyes of the Tory maid, and hoping that the part I had played in the matter of the toast might come to her ears and cause her to give me a smile at our next meeting, I heard the sound of footsteps coming down the passageway.

"There is great danger," said a voice, which I recognised as the landlord's, as they were passing by my door. "Rodolph is stirring up the crowd, and though you might brave the mob, Mistress Jean—" and then the voices died away.

"The mob" and "Mistress Jean." Clearly something must be afoot. Springing from my bed, I swore to myself, that, if anything happened to the Tory maid, I would make Phil Rodolph feel the edge of my sword. Hastily throwing on my clothes, I went to the window and looked out. The night was dark, the sky being full of drifting clouds, through which the moon faintly struggled; everything lay quiet and still in the village and the camp. Steps were heard upon the porch below, and then a horse was brought around from the stables. A moment later a horseman mounted, and I saw a slender figure on the pillion behind him.

"Keep to the south road," said a voice, "they have only one sentry there."

I did not wait to hear more, but slipped downstairs and out of a side door, and the next moment I was running softly through the camp to the outpost on the south road, for one of my own men was stationed there, and I knew that without orders or the countersign no man would pass that way that night. It was well I did, for as I drew near I heard the challenge "Who goes there?" and the answer "A friend."

"Advance, friend, and give the countersign."

"Maryland." But the Tory had missed it, and the next moment the sentry's rifle was at his shoulder, and I knew the cry for the officer of the guard would follow; so I stepped out from the shadow, and the sentry, seeing me, brought his rifle to a salute.

"Lieutenant," he said, "he wants to pass, and has given the wrong countersign."

"Yes," said I, drawing my hat over my eyes, for I did not wish to be recognised by Mistress Jean. "I heard. But I know them; let them pass."

"Certainly, Lieutenant."

"Thank you," said the rider, and a still softer "Thank you" came from his companion. I bowed, but said nothing, and stood there watching them disappear down the dark road until the sound of the horse's hoofs was lost in the distance.

"Queer time of the night to ride, sir," said the sentinel.

"Yes; but they have far to go."

"Kent or Queen Anne's, sir?"

"Down by Bohemia Manor."

"That is where that old Tory Gordon lives; they say they are going to rout him out in the morning for insulting the committee last night. He is up at the inn, there, and Phil Rodolph says he is going to make it hot for him."

"Mere talk, I expect. Good-night."

"Good-night, sir."

I took my way back to the inn, and when I crawled to my room once more and into bed, Dick Ringgold raised himself on his arm and said in a sleepy voice: "What's up, Frisby?"

"Oh, nothing," I replied; "go to sleep." And I soon followed my own advice.

CHAPTER IV

THE RED COCKADE

The stirring notes of the bugle made us spring up in the morning, to find, when we were again downstairs, that every one was talking of the disappearance of Charles Gordon of the Braes.

Master Richard marvelled much at the disappearance of the Tory, and, though I knew it was of the Tory maid he was thinking, I said not a word, but went on with my duties; and manifold they were for many days to come. The drilling of the raw recruits, who, though they were full of fire and *élan*, were not used to the strict obedience of orders, was at first very difficult. But soon there came the spirit and the pride that were to make them the best drilled troops, the dandies and macaronies of the army. And so, with the drilling of recruits and assisting Captain Ramsay in the formation of the regiment, a week passed by before a day came when Dick and I found a few spare hours on our hands. And having certain plans and purposes in view, and not wishing them to be known to Dick, I sat and watched for an opportunity to slip away.

Master Richard, it was evident, had also some plans on foot, for after moving from the chair to the top of a box and then back again, he stretched his arms above his head, and, yawning, said: "I believe I will take a little canter down the south road; come along?"

"No," I replied; "I am going to ride a short distance down the east road."

"All right," said he, and springing from his chair, he went to order his horse. I soon followed, and, having seen Dick well on his way, rode for a short distance on the east road, then turned, rode back, and entered the road which runs along the bank of the Elk, by which we had entered the town on our journey from Kent. As I rode, I hummed a jovial hunting-song and touched Toby with the spur, for I was quite jubilant at having got rid of Dick and so well on the road to my adventure.

My time was short and it was good twelve miles to the Braes, but Toby's sire was a son of old Ranter, and I knew he could do it in an hour and a half. So Toby felt the spur, and I barely noticed the miles as we flew along, until we came to the road that leads south to the Braes. Down this road we turned, and as we were so near the end of our journey I began to think of the reasons and excuses I should give for my visit. Reason! Pshaw! What better reason does a Marylander want than a pair of blue eyes? And if Mistress Jean should so much as demand it by the merest glance of those eyes, I would tell her so. Aye, but she is a Tory and wears the red cockade. True, but the fairer the enemy the more difficult the prize, the greater the glory and effort to win.

And so, having justified my invasion of the stronghold of the Tory, I pricked Toby with the spur and rode on more rapidly, when, on turning a bend in the road where it is intersected by one from the east, whom should I come face to face with but Master Richard? For a moment he stared at me with open mouth, and I at him; then his brow grew dark.

"I thought," he cried; but suddenly the humour of our meeting came over him. Thrusting his hands into his pockets, he broke out into a hearty burst of laughter, and I could do nothing but follow.

"And so, Master Frisby, you rode down the east road."

"And you, methinks, rode down the south." Again our laughter rang through the woods.

"Come," he cried, "which is it to be? So fair a maid deserves two cavaliers, but we would be at sword points within a week, and I do not wish to lose the friendship of Mr. James Frisby of Fairlee."

"A chance has brought us here, so let chance decide."

"Agreed," said Dick, pulling out a sovereign, and with a twitch of the thumb, he sent it high in the air. "Heads, you win. Tails, I win." Then catching it as it fell: "By Jove, you have it. Present my compliments to Mistress Jean," he cried, with a grandiloquent bow, "and tell her how near she came to being Mrs. Dick Ringgold of Hunting Field."

"That I will, Sir Richard." But Dick was gone, and I was left to ride on to the Braes.

A long, rambling house it was, standing white amid the trees, a wide lawn around it stretching down to the creek at its foot; while beyond could be seen the sunlight gleaming on the bay. A quaint, old-fashioned place, the low roof already growing dark with age; the quiet air of ease and comfort brooding over all, making a fitting setting for the quaint, slender little lady that ruled its destinies.

A negro took my horse; another showed me across the broad hall, with its hunting whips and trophies on the wall, to the parlour, and there I awaited the coming of the Tory maid. And as I sat there, gently stroking the toe of my boot with my whip, and thinking of that night at the inn, of that soft "Thank you" on the old south road, I heard the soft swish of her skirts, and, looking up, saw Mistress Jean standing in the doorway. A beautiful picture it was, like some old portrait of Lely's, the maid standing there framed in the old oak. And I, though I had been to the balls at the Governor's house the winter before, and was therefore a man of the world, sat staring for a moment. But she advanced, and I was on my feet with a low and sweeping bow.

"Father is away," said she, "but in his name I wish to thank you for defending us at the inn that night."

So she knew.

"It was to save the honour of Maryland gentlemen," I replied modestly. "Heretofore they have not fought in mobs. But will you not thank me for yourself?"

"When you turn loyalist, yes," said she.

"Almost thou persuadest me to become a traitor."

"You are that already," she said with spirit.

"Yes, that is the way they have written 'Patriot' since Tyranny first stalked across the world. But patriot or traitor, Mistress Jean, I have already won one 'Thank you,' and I hope some day to win another."

"Won one 'Thank you'—when and where?" and she looked at me with wide open eyes.

Now every Marylander will admit that there are no more gallant fellows in the world than we are, and if any one chooses to dispute it, well and good, we are willing to cross swords with him any day, and so reprove him for his recklessness. Indeed, we have been called with truth the Gascons of the South, and, like those gallant gentlemen of old France, we have never hidden our light under a bushel, to use a homely phrase; and so when I saw Mistress Jean's air of surprise, the spirit of my race came over me.

"Yes," I replied, "it was the sweetest 'Thank you' I ever heard."

Again the mystified look.

"But where?" said she again.

"It was rather dark," I replied, "and the clouds were drifting across the sky, and you, I am afraid, did not know who it was who received that soft 'Thank you.'"

"Were you the Lieutenant?"

I bowed.

"Oh," she said, and she stamped her tiny foot, "if you were only not a rebel!"

"But even rebels have their uses."

Thus it was we became good friends in spite of the traitor stamped upon my brow. Ere I knew it, the time approached when

I had to mount and ride. But before I left, her soft hand rested for a moment in mine.

"We march in a few days," said I, "to the North, to the Leaguer of Boston. There will be fighting there and bloody work. Can I not carry a single token?"

Her nimble fingers flew to her hair, and took from thence a blood-red rose, and pinned it to my coat.

"There," said she, "my red cockade;" and turning quickly, she ran into the house.

CHAPTER V

SIR SQUIRE OF TORY DAMES

"Well, Sir Squire of Tory Dames, did she smile on you?" The voice was harsh and rasping; looking across the table, I saw the sneer upon his lips. I had but entered a moment before the dining-room of the inn, after my long ride, and was about to take my seat, when Rodolph's sneering question made me pause.

"That is more than you could ever win, my Mighty Lord from Nowhere," I retorted. At this there was a laugh from those about. An angry flush showed through even his dark and swarthy skin; for, being a burly bully of the border, he liked not being bearded thus by a youth.

"You damned impudent puppy!" he cried, rising.

But there stood a glass at my right hand, full to the brim, and ere he could say another word the red wine flew across the table straight into his face.

"Take that!" I cried, "with the compliments of James Frisby of Fairlee!"

A dozen men were now around us, and Rodolph, spluttering through the wine and swearing many oaths, demanded to be released from the hands upon his shoulders, shouting that he would shoot me like a dog.

"It will give me pleasure to let you have an opportunity," I replied coolly. "It will be a rare chance for you to become a gentleman."

And so, still muttering and swearing, his friends took him from the room, while I took my seat at the table. But I was not allowed to eat my meal in peace; for many gentlemen came to offer their services and to thank me. Rodolph's overbearing manners had long been unpopular among them, and the wonder was that he had not been forced to fight before. But I was determined that Dick should be my second, and so, thanking them all for their kind offers, I placed my hand on Dick's shoulder, and we went out together amid a volley of advice and friendly warning.

Half an hour later, as I was examining my sword and Dick his pistols, there came a rap on my door, and two gentlemen entered; one was Captain Brooke, the other Lieutenant Barry of the Line.

"Lieutenant Frisby," said Captain Brooke, as he advanced and bowed, "it is my painful duty to deliver you this challenge."

"It is a pleasure to receive it from your hands," I replied, returning his courtesy. "Lieutenant Ringgold and Harry Gresham of Kent will act as my seconds, permit me to refer you to them."

Dick now went out with them to Harry Gresham's room near by, where they would be safe from interruption, Gresham having volunteered with Dick to be one of my seconds, and I went on polishing my sword, waiting for the issue. At last Dick came back.

"Well," he cried, "it is all settled. You are to fight tomorrow morning at sunrise down in the little meadow below the creek."

"Swords, I suppose?"

"No; pistols. I insisted on swords at first, it being our privilege; but Captain Brooke said that Rodolph had broken his arm the year before, and that it was still too weak to fight with. So I waived the swords and agreed to the pistols."

"It is not quite as gentlemanly a weapon, but just as deadly. I have put a bullet through the head of a wild duck flying, and I think I can hit Phil Rodolph."

"That you can," said Dick.

It was a bright, clear morning as we slipped out of the inn on our way to the little meadow. The eastern sky was already tinged with crimson, and the blood-red lances across the heavens told of the coming dawn. The air was fresh and cool as it blew up the river from the bay, and our lungs drew in great draughts of it as we felt the breeze in our faces.

"A splendid morning to die on," said Harry Gresham.

"And to live on, too," I replied.

"Stop your croaking, Gresham," put in Dick Ringgold. We walked on silently to the meadow, where we found that we were the first to arrive.

Though I have stood on many a field of honour since that day, though I have felt the bullet tearing and burning its way through the flesh, and the sudden, sharp pain of the sword thrust, I shall never forget that encounter on the meadow beside the Elk, when I first faced the muzzle of a hostile pistol, and knew that the will behind it sought my life.

It was not fear that I felt as I stood there, waiting for the coming of my adversary, for fear has always been foreign to my family, but a sort of secret elation. For that day, if I survived, though the down upon my lip was as yet imperceptible, I could take my place as a man among men. No longer would my boyish face keep me out of the councils of my elders, but I would have the right to take my stand and ruffle it with the best of them all. I was there to win my spurs as a man and a duellist, and to show to all the world that I had the courage of my race. For then, as it has ever been in the fair province of Maryland, we love above all else courage in a man; and so it was I waited with impatience Rodolph's approach, for it meant the casting off of the boy and the making of the man.

We did not have long to wait, for Rodolph and his seconds soon followed us down the path, and each party saluted. Then Captain Brooke and Dick Ringgold measured off the paces, and threw for the choice of positions. Dick won, and I found myself standing near a small sapling, with my back to the rising sun, which as yet had not climbed over the tree tops, and so did not interfere with Rodolph's position. Facing me, twelve paces away, stood Rodolph, his dark, swarthy face darker, more Indian-like, and forbidding than ever; behind him stretched away the small glade, and the smooth green waters of the river, as they wound their way between the tall forests on either side. I remember watching a wild duck as he went swiftly flying down the Elk, when Dick Ringgold's "Are you ready?" suddenly recalled me to my position. "Yes," I nodded. Then came the even counting, "One, two;" but ere "two" had been uttered, I saw the flash of Rodolph's pistol, and felt the sharp pain of the bullet tearing its way into my side. While I, taken by surprise at such rank treachery, fired not so accurately as usual, and my bullet clipped his ear. Dick's sword was out in an instant, and I verily believe he would have run Rodolph through on the spot, as it was his duty and right to do, so base was the crime of firing before the time—a thing that had never been known among Maryland gentlemen before. But seeing me reel, he came to my assistance, and threw his arm around me.

"Tie me to the sapling, Dick," said I, "and give me one more shot."

"But no gentleman should fight with such a scoundrel!" cried Dick hotly.

"I waive that, just one more shot."

So, with Harry Gresham's assistance, they took Dick's sash and tied me to the sapling, and in this way enabled me to keep an upright position. Captain Brooke had come forward to inquire as to my injury, but Dick met him and demanded another exchange of shots. "My principal," he said, "waives the treachery that places your principal beyond the pale of men of honour. But," continued Dick, "if he should dare to fire again before the time, I will shoot him down where he stands."

Captain Brooke flushed, and though we saw that it was painful to him as a man of honour to be the second of such a principal, he could do nothing but accept. "I will shoot him down myself," said he, "if he dares again to do it."

He then returned to his party, and we saw by his angry gestures that he was warning Rodolph of the penalty if he should a second time transgress the rules of honour.

Again we faced, and I could feel the strength ebbing fast from me, but I could see that Rodolph's face was pale, even through his swarthy skin. "One, two, three, Fire," came again the fateful words; but I had nerved myself for the final effort, and glancing down the polished barrel, I fired, at the same moment that Rodolph's pistol rang out.

For a moment I saw him standing there, and then he lurched forward, with his arms in the air, and fell face downward as the mortally wounded do. With that there came a mist before my eyes, my hand fell to my side, and I remembered nothing more. They told me afterward that they carried me to the inn in the village, Captain Brooke assisting, after they had seen that Rodolph was dead. "Leave him there for awhile," said the Captain, as he came to assist Dick in my removal. "The dog had a better death than he deserved."

CHAPTER VI

A TALE IS TOLD

I lay there at the inn, I do not know how long, but they told me afterward it was for many days, hanging on the brink between life and death, until one day I heard in my dreams the music of the fife and the rattle of the drums, and awoke to life and hope again. The sunlight was streaming through the south window across the counterpane of the bed, and outside could be heard the steady tread of marching men.

"What troops are those?" I asked somewhat hazily, for I was still on the borderland of dreams.

"They are the Maryland Line marching away to the North to join General Washington."

"Marching to the North? Then I must join them." And I tried to rise in my bed, for it came back to me with a rush that I was a Lieutenant in the Line. But strong hands pushed me gently back upon my pillow, and I recognised now the voice of my nurse, Mrs. McLean.

"No, no, Mr. Frisby; be still. You are a regular little bantam, but your spurs are clipped for some time yet."

"Why, what is the matter, Mrs. McLean? How did I come here?"

"Law bless the boy!" said the good old soul. "He has clean forgot."

But the dull pain in my side soon brought back to me that clear, fresh morning on the bank of the Elk, and for a moment I lay still.

"Did I kill Rodolph?" I asked.

"That you did, lad; and no man deserved it more."

Then I heard a heavy step in the passageway outside, and then a lighter one. The next moment the door opened and I saw my mother, more pale and fairy-like than ever, and behind her came Captain Ramsay, bluff and hearty, but looking very solemn at that moment. But they saw the news on Mrs. McLean's good-natured face, and when I spoke to my lady, the old-time happy look came back again, as she came to my bedside and kissed me, while the great voice of the Captain came hearty and strong.

"Aye, lad, I told them that you would pull through; make a gallant fight, my boy, and you will have a shot at the redcoats yet."

"But, Captain, you are marching away without me."

"You will be in time for the fighting, never worry; lie still and get well. Half the young men in the Line are envying you, you rogue, for becoming a hero before them all." And the Captain took my hand, and bade me good-bye, for he must hurry away to join his regiment.

A few minutes later there came the clank of a sword and a hurried step, and then the door burst open and in marched Master Dick in all the glory of his full regimentals. And so brave was the show that he made in his cocked hat, scarlet coat, with its facings of buff, and the long clanking sword, that I longed to spring up and don my own then and there. But my mother's finger on her lip caused him to stop the cheery greeting, and he came forward on his tiptoes, holding his sword carefully to keep it from clanking, for by this time I was growing weak again. Master Dick shook my hand gently and murmured, "Cheer up, old fellow, you will soon be with us again," but I could only give him a slight smile, for I was again on the borderland of dreams. Dick stood for awhile looking down on me; then he, too, had to depart. Gradually the steady tramp of marching feet died away, and everything became quiet and still again.

The days passed by, week followed week, and though at first I gained strength but slowly, the process seeming a long and dreary one, the vigour of a youthful frame soon asserted itself, and I could feel the returning tide of health and strength. But as yet I lay there upon the great four-post bed, with my mother sitting near by, her dear face bending over the embroidery frame, as her deft fingers weaved beautiful designs with the silk. As I lay there, I would wander back again to that day before the duel, to the swift challenging glance of a pair of blue eyes as a blood-red rose was pinned to my coat. But that was so long ago, years it seemed to me, away back in the past, a memory as it were of a fairy tale heard from the lips of a grandmother before the big open fire in the great hall on a winter night; a fairy tale, aye, and she the Princess, with her blue eyes and hair of waving brown, with her step as light as the dew-drop, and her voice as low and soft as the breath of the Southern breeze in the spring; and then I would be her Prince Charming, with my coal-black horse. But, pshaw! I am becoming a child again; whereas I am a man, who has fought his duel as becomes a man, with a right to the sword by his side. And yet those blue eyes, what fate was in store for them? And would their challenging glance ever meet mine again? But here my mother stopped the trend of my thoughts for a moment.

"James," she said, "John Cotton tells me that an old darky

comes to inquire for you every night. Strange, is it not? We know so few people here."

"Yes," I replied. "Does John Cotton know who he is?"

"No; he refuses to tell, and all John Cotton can find out is that he leaves town by the river road. He appears to be a stranger to all the other darkies, and nobody seems to know him."

By the river road! Could it possibly be, then, that it was the Tory maid who sent those many miles to see if I were in the land of the living or the dead? Ah, it was too pleasant a thing to dream of; too pleasant to have it shattered by the rough hand of fact. And so I said dreamily, "It is only one of John Cotton's stories, I suppose."

Yet I would not have believed it otherwise for all of John Cotton's weight in gold. Thus it was I was thinking one day of the Tory maid, when the door opened, and a tall, dignified gentleman came in—the man who had stood by my side that day when with drawn sword I held the door against Rodolph and his followers—Mr. Lambert Wilmer of the White House in Kent.

He came forward and greeted me with many kind phrases. While he sat talking to me of the duel and its cause, I thought of that great burst of laughter when he told Rodolph to put up his sword, as by this time he should have had enough of Gordon of the Braes, and I asked the reason for it all.

"It is a long story, lad," said he, "but I will tell it to you."

Then he told me how, many years before, Mistress Margaret Nicholson had been the loveliest girl in Kent, and the belle of the whole shore, and how there was not a bachelor within three counties who did not seek her as his bride, or who would not have sold his soul for a glance of her eyes or the soft pressure of her hand; and how when James Rodolph of Charlestown Hundred came riding down from Cecil and boasted of his wealth, his horses, and his slaves, swearing that he would win her or no one would, the suitors stood aside to see how he would fare with this the proudest of Kent beauties. To their dismay, he seemed to prosper well, until one day there disembarked from a vessel that came sailing up the broad Chester a young gentleman of distinguished appearance, who asked his way to Radcliffe, the home of the Nicholsons.

"Now, the Nicholsons, as you know," said Mr. Wilmer, "are Scotch, and this young gentleman was Scotch, for his accent betrayed him, and we, thinking he might be a cousin and have brought news from over the water, welcomed him, and showed him the way to Radcliffe. He, though he was very reserved, told us that he had indeed come from over the sea, and bore a letter to the Nicholsons, who were old friends of his family, but of himself he would say no more. And so, when he strode off, we turned to Captain Hezekiah Brown of the Maid of Perth, who was a man who delighted to talk. From him we learned that his name was Gordon, and that there was a mystery about him, as people suspected him of being one of the young chiefs who had led that famous clan in the recent rebellion against the King. But this we held not to his injury, for there were still many lovers of the White Rose in the fair province of Maryland, and we afterward welcomed him the more heartily for it. From the advent of the stranger the good fortune of James Rodolph began to wane; for the rich planter of the border, with his wild and boisterous manners, was no match for the Scottish cavalier. It is true that he was penniless, but he was very handsome, of distinguished manners and address, and when it became known that he was out in 'forty-five' the mantle of romance that fell around Prince Charles was shared as well by him, and he became the hero of many a pair of fair eyes.

"James Rodolph soon saw this, and his hatred grew from day to day, as his rival became more successful. One day there was a quarrel, and next morning, upon the smooth, sandy shore of the river, they met and fought it out. Rodolph was fiery, quick, and fierce; Gordon cool and steady; until Rodolph, growing weary and desperate, tried a foul and dangerous stroke, to find his rapier flying through the air, to fall with a splash into the river.

"'I would not stain my blade by killing you,' said Gordon; and turning with the other gentlemen who had seen the foul stroke, he walked away, leaving him there.

"And so it was that Rodolph came back to Cecil with a blot upon his name, and Gordon married the maid, and became in time the owner of the Braes, for she was an heiress as well as a great beauty. From that time has grown the feud which we may some day see the end of. And that is why the people laughed and Rodolph slunk away. For the old story is known throughout the shore, and Rodolph proved, in his fight with you, the bad blood in his veins. It never does to cross the white blood with the red, for the treachery of the Indian will taint the race for generations."

Thus it was, by the light of this old tale of thirty years before, I saw and read the cause and reason of it all—of his fatal course, of our quarrel, and of the meeting by the banks of the river Elk.

CHAPTER VII

THE DEFIANCE OF THE TORY

A few weeks later I was up and out, fast gaining strength and courage for the long ride to the northward to join the gallant fellows of the Maryland Line, who had taken up their line of march soon after the accident befell me. And though I was eager to be off, the surgeon would not let me go, and so, until I could gather strength for the long journey, I served as best I could my country and the commands of the Committee of Public Safety sitting at the Head of Elk. Thus it was I rode one day by the side of Edward Veasey, High Sheriff of the county of Cecil, carrying the writ and command of the Committee of Public Safety to Charles Gordon of the Braes, now a suspected Tory and a malcontent. And as I rode by the side of the High Sheriff on this most unpleasant task, I longed to turn back and let the Sheriff ride on alone; but duty held me as a point of honour. For as it was, I was carrying I knew not what ruin and destruction to the roof of the very house that once had received me as a guest and that sheltered the fairest eyes that had ever gazed in mine. And now I was to appear before that house as the bearer of ill-tidings. Ah, duty often wears a gruesome countenance; yet it is a sign of courage to face this duty down, and I sat more firmly in my saddle and rode nearer to the High Sheriff. He was a stern and determined man; he was short of stature, stout of frame, and sat his powerful horse like the fox-hunter that he was. But, though it was the height of summer, and the hills and the forests were green, the air laden with the odour of flowers, and the streams full and rushing, there was anything but a smile on the High Sheriff's face. For though he was no friend to Gordon of the Braes, he liked not the errand on which he rode, and would gladly have turned his horse's head with me.

"If they want to fight," said he to me, "why don't they join the Maryland Line and leave men alone who are disposed to be quiet? They will have enough to do in repulsing the redcoats, and should not stir up opposition in the rear of our armies, which this persecution of private individuals will certainly do. I wish some other carried this writ, and I was with the lads fighting in the North."

"Aye, so do I, but it is the order of the committee," said I grimly.

"True, and as such must be obeyed."

We had come to where the ferry crosses the Elk, and hailing it we were soon on the south bank and taking up again the road that leads to the Braes. Over the hills and dales of Cecil, the forest, streams, and rivers, the soft warm sunlight played, and nature blessed with lavish hand the harvest of the year. Seldom had she been more pleasing, the earth bursting with flowers and the very trees welcoming with outstretched arms the soft breezes wafted from the bay. And then, after some hours' travelling, we came to the Braes and I saw again the long rambling house amid the trees. I took a firmer grip upon my sense of duty and rode on. The clatter of our horses' hoofs as we rode up to the door announced us. A moment later Charles Gordon came through the open doorway on to the porch. Though I had seen him before, it seemed to me, as I saw him standing there, with the memory of the old tale in my mind, that I saw not the Tory, but one of those figures of romance that stepped out from the mystery and the haze of the North, when Prince Charles raised his standard in the Highlands, one of those heroic men who drew swords with Wallace and with Bruce, rallied with Montrose, and went to death with a cheer behind Bonnie Dundee at Killiecrankie, of such gallant bearing and bold and open countenance was he.

"What brings you here, Mr. Sheriff, riding so fast?"

"I come, Charles Gordon of the Braes," replied the Sheriff, "to serve on you the writ and summons of the Committee of Public Safety." And here he unfolded the summons and read aloud, sitting on his horse as he was:

> "*Whereas*, Great complaints have this day been made against Charles Gordon of the Braes, for that he has infamously reflected on the membership of this Committee and the deputies of this county who lately attended the Provincial Convention,
>
> "These are therefore requiring the said Charles Gordon of the Braes that he appear before this Committee, at the house of Thomas Savin at the Head of Elk, tomorrow at two o'clock P.M., to answer unto said complaints.
>
> "Hereto fail not on your peril.
>
> "JAMES RODOLPH, Chairman.
>
> "TO CHARLES GORDON of the Braes."

Then spoke Charles Gordon:

"Go tell those who sent you, Mr. Sheriff, that if they wish to see Charles Gordon they will have to come to the Braes to do so; that I will give them a right warm welcome, as my plantation is large enough to hold them all; but that if any of their rascally crew dare to approach the house, there will be lives lost; for I say to you, Mr. Sheriff, as I have said before and will say again, that James Rodolph and his committee are a set of infamous scoundrels, who have usurped such power and authority in troublous times as the King himself would not dare to claim. Tell them that I am at their defiance, that I do not recognise their authority, and that I have as much contempt for them as I have for their dogs."

The old gentleman, for he must have been nearly sixty, looked splendid in his wrath, as he denounced the Committee of Public Safety. The ring in his voice told that the ire of the Scot was rising.

For an instant the High Sheriff hesitated, as if he would turn and go, but then he said:

"Charles Gordon, I spoke to you a moment ago as an officer of the law. I speak to you now as one who does not wish you an injury. Obey the order of the committee, and I will see that you have fair speech before it. Refuse and you will be declared a traitor and an outlaw, and the edict will go forth through all the province that no man shall buy of you, that no man shall sell to you, and he that shows you kindness will become an outlaw like yourself."

Charles Gordon laughed.

"Do you think I care a snap of a finger for their edict? There has not been a generation of my family that has not been at the Horn at Edinburgh for high treason. Do you think that I care when my neck has been on the block for the part I took at Preston Pans and Culloden? Go frighten the children with their edicts, but not an old Scot who has seen the claymores flash and led the charge for the King who is over the sea."

"If you fought against the father, why not against the son?"

"A fair question deserves a fair answer. When my head was on the block my life was saved by the intercession of the Duchess of Gordon, but upon conditions, and those conditions are these: That I should nevermore bear arms against the King, that I should leave the realm of Scotland, sail across the sea to the province of Maryland, there remain and never return. So, though I love not the King nor his race, I will not draw sword against him, for never yet has a Gordon broken faith with friend or foe. Yet for all that I will not take up arms for the King's cause unless I am forced to do so by such rascals as compose your Committee of Public Safety."

"So be it, then, but I wish it were otherwise," said the Sheriff; and, turning, we rode away, leaving him standing there. As I entered the woods I looked back again, my eyes searching every window in the old house, but never a sign of the Tory maid did I see.

CHAPTER VIII

THE BLACK COCKADE

It was two o'clock next day when we rode up to the house where the Committee of Public Safety held its meetings, dismounted, and entered the room. Six gentlemen sat at the long table, and the room was crowded with hangers-on. They were men who stayed behind while the others went to the war; they fought the fight with their tongues, with writs of forfeiture for high treason, became great statesmen, and in time aspired to become members of the committee. How the worthy High Sheriff regarded them could be seen by the manner in which he brushed past them to stand before the committee.

"What right have you to talk of liberty and of freedom, if you will not fight for it? Why are you not with Howard, Gist, Smallwood, and the other heroes who are making the name of the Maryland Line ring through the army?" he would ask, and they would turn away.

The burly form and dark, swarthy face of the Chairman dominated the committee. As we entered and stood before him his dark eyes flashed.

"Do you bring the body of Charles Gordon with you?" he demanded.

"No; I do not. I bring his defiance, instead;" and the High Sheriff delivered the message of Charles Gordon to the committee.

The committee glanced from one to another, and there was a big stir in the room. Then the Chairman was on his feet.

"By a thousand devils," he swore, "Charles Gordon shall suffer for this. I will not stop until the Braes is razed to the ground, and I have driven him from the province. He is a Tory and a traitor, and a danger to the peace of the county. He will be up in arms next. Mr. Sheriff, summon a posse and ride to the Braes and bring us the body of Charles Gordon, dead or alive."

"You will not accept the invitation to go to the Braes yourself, then?" asked the High Sheriff gravely, though there was the suggestion of a smile around the corners of his mouth.

The Chairman hesitated. "No," he said; "it is absolutely necessary for the welfare of the county of Cecil that we should remain where we are and not engage in any brawls or tumults, for if we are killed who will take our places?"

"That is true," said the High Sheriff ironically, "but have you considered, gentlemen, that Charles Gordon's wife was of the Nicholsons of Kent, who, as you know, are the leaders of the patriots in that county? How will they like it when they hear of your burnings and your razings?"

The Chairman frowned. "You are right," he said; "we must proceed about it in a legal way, which is slow but sure. Mr. Clerk, institute proceedings against Charles Gordon for the forfeiture of his lands for high treason, and meanwhile we will publish him throughout the province as a Tory and a traitor. We will teach this Charles Gordon and all Tories what it means to contemn the authority and dignity of this province and its committee."

And then applause broke out from the crowd; but the High Sheriff, who left the room with me, shrugged his shoulders and said: "If they had half of the courage of that Scot they would not be loafing around here, applauding James Rodolph. I am tired of it; I am going to resign and go to the front." He was as good as his word, for that very day he resigned the office of High Sheriff of the county of Cecil, packed his saddle-bags, gathered some volunteers about him, and rode away to the North, becoming in time a noted officer. But it was not until the month of August of that year that I was ready to follow him and felt equal to the length of the journey. On the night of the day before I took my departure I called John Cotton and ordered him to saddle Toby.

John Cotton received the order with wide-open eyes, as it was growing somewhat late.

"Fo' de Lord's sake, Mars Jim, what do you want Toby fo'? It's after ten o'clock."

"Ask no questions, you black rascal, and bring Toby around in a hurry."

Then his eyes fell on a cluster of red roses on my table, and a broad grin crept from ear to ear.

"Sartin, Mars Jim, sartin;" and he was out of the door before my flying boot could repay the impertinence of that grin. A few minutes later I slipped out of the house to the stables, and, mounting Toby, was soon riding out of the silent town, having hit that rascal John Cotton across the shoulders with my whip for the snickering laugh he could not restrain as I was riding off.

Have you ever ridden by the silent river after the night has fallen, and when it is far advanced? The great trees, rising far above you like the vaulted arch of a cathedral, overhanging the path down which you ride; the smooth flowing waters of the river, the towering dark mass on the farther shore, and over all the glorious moon shining down flooding everything with its silvery light, weird and fantastic, glinting now like polished steel upon the waters, now deepening the shadows of the forest, or flooding again with its glorious radiance some wide and sweeping stretch of water. And then, the unearthly silence of it all, the mournful howl of the wolf in the hills, and the piercing shrill cry of the wildcat, like that of a child tortured by the demons of hell; then the horror of its beauty, its stillness and its loneliness, comes over you; nervous chills become distinctly apparent, and you put spurs to your horse and ride on more rapidly, and the night is broken first by your whistle and then by your song. So it was, as I rode by the banks of the Elk, that night in early August, and my voice rang across the waters, as I sang the old Highland ballad:

The Gordons cam', and the Gordons ran,
And they were stark and steady,
And aye the word among them a'
Was, Gordons, keep you ready.

A ballad that I heard a young girl sing one day not long before. Thus the length of my ride passed quickly away until Toby felt the soft grass under his feet as I rode silently across the lawn. Her window was high, it is true, but it was open to admit the fresh, cool breeze from the bay, and then I had not thrown quoits in my youth not to be able to surmount so small a difficulty. So I fastened a black cockade amid the blood-red of the roses, and, rising in my stirrups, threw them firmly and gently, and saw them rise in the air, top the window-sill, and fall with a slight thud upon the floor. I did not wait for more, but turned and rode away; but it seemed to me that as I gained the shadow of the forest and looked back I saw the faint suggestion of a girlish form standing at the open window. I looked once again and rode on.

When morning came, I bade good-bye to my mother, mounted my black colt Toby, and rode away to join the Maryland Line, which was marching now from Boston, to meet the British before New York. As that day I crossed the line into the province of Delaware, I saw nailed to a great oak the proclamation of the Committee of Public Safety, denouncing Charles Gordon as a Tory and a traitor, and calling upon all persons to have no dealings with him, either in public or private, at their peril. And thus it was at every cross-roads in the county of Cecil, and in all the counties to the south and west, the edict had gone forth.

Now in Maryland, as I have said before, we love, above all

else, courage in a man, and so I rode under the oak, and tore down the proclamation, for I knew the courage of Charles Gordon, Tory though he was. I knew also that the proceedings of forfeiture had been instituted against him in the High Court of the Province, and that ere I set foot on the soil of Maryland again, he would be driven from the province, and it was for this that I paid this courtesy to the courage of an enemy, as I left my native plains behind me.

It was a long road for a lad, but the people received me with open arms and urged me on when I told them whither I was riding. After several days of travelling along the shore of the Delaware and across the low-lying plains of New Jersey, I came to the banks of the Hudson, and saw across the water the great city of New York, its clustering houses and steeples. And then it was not long before I was on the ferry that conveyed me across the river, and heard the sharp ring of the pavement under my horse's feet as I rode toward the great common where lay the encampment of the troops. It was near twelve o'clock when I came to the camp of the patriots and asked my way of an officer to the quarters of the Maryland Line.

"You must be a stranger," he said, "or you would know that the Maryland Line always has the place of honour in the camp;" and he showed me where their quarters lay.

I felt aglow with pride when I heard this tribute to my countrymen. I thanked him and rode on. A few minutes later I was among them. The great voice of the Captain was giving me greeting; Dick Ringgold's hand was on my shoulder, as he took charge of me; and many of my kith and kin, old friends and neighbours who belonged to that famous corps, came forward to greet and welcome me to the camp. Thus, after many days of sickness and of travel, I took my place among the men who were about to face the great storm. True, at the time quiet reigned all along our front, which lay over beyond the heights of Brooklyn; but hot work was soon expected, as the British fleet had been seen in the offing, and it was only a question of time when the army would be landed and the attack begun.

CHAPTER IX

THE RED TIDE OF BLOOD

Spruce Macaronies, and pretty to see,
Tidy and dapper and gallant were we;
Blooded, fine gentlemen, proper and tall,
Bold in a fox-hunt and gay at a ball;

Tralara! Tralara! now praise we the Lord,
For the clang of His call and the flash of His sword.
Tralara! Tralara! now forward to die;
For the banner, hurrah! and for sweethearts, good-bye!

JOHN WILLIAMSON PALMER.

It was on the 22d day of August that the rumour flew through the camp that the enemy had landed and was preparing to attack. But the hours flew by, and still no orders came, until the Line became restless, and the fear grew that the fight would begin before we could reach the field of battle. The sun began to sink over the Heights of Harlem when an aide rode into our lines. It was Tench Tilghman, who swung his hat and shouted as he went by: "You will have warm work in a day or two, boys!"

We gave him a yell in reply, and started with renewed interest the preparations for the coming fight. A few minutes later came the orders that we were to march at dawn. The men received the news joyfully, and it was wonderful to see the change in their bearing; for while the doubt hung over them, they were restless and murmuring was heard all through the camp; but now all was laughter and gaiety. They prepared for the fight as one would prepare for the next county ball or a fox-hunt on the morrow.

The stirring notes of the bugle ringing over the camp brought me to my feet with a bound, and I looked out of the tent to see a heavy mist over everything, and hear the sound of men's voices coming through it all around me. It does not take a soldier long to don his uniform, and I was soon out attending to my duties. At seven o'clock we were on our march to the ferry, crossing the East River at the foot of the main street of the small town of Brooklyn; then we took a road leading over a creek called Gowanus, and knew that we were marching to guard the right of the American line. Low-lying hills, heavily wooded, lay before us; it was in these woods that our line was called to a halt, and we took up our position for the battle. We lay there several days, with constant rumours flying through the camp of the enemy's advance, but yet they would not come.

It was on the morning of the 27th of August that the great battle of Long Island, so disastrous for the patriot forces, broke upon us. The scattering shots of the skirmishers first made us spring to arms; then the sharp rattle of the musketry of Atlee's men and the boom of Carpenter's cannon on our immediate right told that the enemy was pushing them hard. Then through the forest trees came the line of the British advance. The fire extended along our whole front, while far over, to our left came the distant roar of cannon and musketry.

"They are having a hot time over there," said Dick, "but why don't these fellows charge us?"

"They will charge us soon enough," I replied. But it seemed as if they never would, for what promised to be an attack along our whole line dwindled down to a mere exchange of shots. Hour after hour went by, and yet they never advanced beyond a certain point except when a company or so would dash forward and a sharp skirmish would break forth for a moment or two, and then die away again. But far over to our left the sound of the battle came rolling nearer and nearer, telling the tale of Sullivan's men being driven in.

"I do not like that," said Dick. "They are doing all the fighting, while we are merely exchanging courtesies with our friends six hundred yards away. Hello! There comes news."

I looked behind us to a small hill, where Lord Stirling stood with his staff, and saw Tench Tilghman riding up at full speed. There was a hurried movement among the staff, and Stirling's glasses swept the country to our left and rear. A moment later an order was given and the aides came dashing down our lines, and then, to our disgust, came the order to retire.

"Retreat!" cried one of the men. "Why, we haven't begun to fight yet!"

"Steady, men," cried Captain Ramsay; "you form the rear guard and must hold the enemy in check," for they were beginning to advance as the regiments on each side of us withdrew. Then we began slowly to withdraw, but there came an aide riding swiftly to Major Gist. Pennsylvania and Delaware regiments took our place in the rear, and we were marched rapidly to the front. The heavy woods had heretofore prevented our seeing what was taking place, but now that we had come out to the opening a wild scene of terror and dismay lay before us. Gowanus Creek, deep and unfordable, with its sullen tide rising fast, lay like a great ugly serpent across our path, while over the meadow and far in our front the broken streams of fugitives were swarming, flying toward the bridge at the mill, the only hope of crossing Gowanus Creek. And as I looked, to my horror, the mill and the bridge burst into flames, catching the routed army as it were between the rising tide and the advancing legions of the victorious English. Then, as we watched it, a rumour grew and spread through the ranks, as such things will in battle, that a New England Colonel had fired the bridge to save himself and his regiment. How we cursed New England then, and swore that if we ever escaped we would have our reckoning with her and her people.

"There they come!" cried Dick at my side, pointing to where a large stone house crowned a hill immediately in the rear and commanded the whole field of the terror-stricken fugitives.

I saw the brilliant scarlet of their coats as they took possession of the hill and prepared to open fire.

"They will have to be driven from there or we are lost," I answered.

Then, as the prospect looked the darkest and the long line of the British formed to make their last advance, Lord Stirling rode up to our line.

"Men of Maryland!" he shouted, "charge that hill, hold Cornwallis in check and save the army!"

We answered with a yell, as he sprang from his horse to lead us.

Ah, I shall never forget the pride with which we stepped out of the mass of flying fugitives, four hundred Marylanders, the greatest dandies and bluest blood in all the army, for this, the proudest service of the day. We formed for the charge as if on the drill ground; our evolutions and lines were perfect, and would have done credit to the grenadiers of the later empire. Stirling's sword was in the air, the drums were beating the charge, when there broke from the throats of our Marylanders the wild, thrilling yell of the southern provinces, and we leaped to the charge up the long hill, straight into the face of Cornwallis's army, a handful against thousands. Up, up the hill we dashed. A fire as of hell broke upon us and rattled and roared about our ears, thinning our ranks and strewing our pathway with the dead. Men fell to the right and to the left of me, and I strode across the bodies of the slain in my path; but still, over the roar of the cannon and the rattle of musketry, high and shrill rose the yell of the charging line. We swept up the hill, the crest was gained, and the British fell back before us, when we were met by a sheet of flame, a storm of lead and smoke and fire. We were raised as it were in the air and held there gasping for breath, and then we were swept back down the hill, struggling desperately to gain a foothold to make a stand.

Again we saw Stirling glance over the meadow and the marsh behind us as we re-formed our line. His voice came ringing down our ranks.

"Once again, men of Maryland."

Once again! Aye, we knew how to answer that call, for the bodies of our comrades lay dotting the long hillside.

"Once again, and charge home!" cried Ramsay.

We sprang to the charge, and wilder, shriller, fiercer, more terrible, rose the yell—the yell of vengeance that seemed to pick the line up bodily and hurl it up the hill through the scorching, blistering storm and hail of lead, fire, and smoke. I remembered naught till the crest was gained, and Edward Veasey crying, "Charge home! Charge home!" and we dashed in upon the scarlet line. Ah me, for a moment, then it was glorious, as steel met steel, and we drove them, ten times our number, back, and rolled them up against the house and forced them off the plain. And then our hands were on the ugly muzzles of the guns, and Edward Veasey, springing on the carriage, cheered on his men. But ere it had died on his lips, so desperate was the struggle, the English Captain of the guns fired, and Veasey fell. I was but a dozen steps away, and, seeing Veasey fall, I dashed through the press of bayonets to where the English Captain fought.

"Another one!" he cried, as we met face to face.

"Yes, and the last;" and our swords met.

"No time for that!" cried a voice at my side; then there was a flash, and the Englishman fell back into the arms of his men, and the guns were won for an instant. But only for an instant. Our men melted away under the storm of lead from the Cortelyou house, and the weight of the advancing regiments forced us back to the crest of the hill. Then slowly, step by step, down the hill they forced us, until we rested once more at its foot.

But still the meadow, the marsh, and the creek were black with the mass of flying men seeking eagerly, desperately to escape, while between them and the victorious British stretched the ranks of the Maryland Line, now sadly thinned, for one-third of our men were dyeing the long dank grass with their blood. But that line, thin as it was, closed up the wide gaps in the ranks with as jaunty a step and as gallant a carriage as when they first stepped out for the charge. Their faces looked grim, it is true, for with the smoke and the fire, and the blood and the dust, the genius of battle had sketched thereon.

For a few minutes we rested at the foot of the hill, for we knew that our work was not half done, and until the last fugitive was over Gowanus Creek we must check the British advance. A glance from Lord Stirling told us to charge, as he pointed up the long hill with his sword.

Again there came the answering yell, the requiem for many a gallant soul, and the line once more swung forward to breast the hill. Up the long hill we toiled again, straight into the teeth of the fire.

Again we gained the crest and fought them, man to man; again by weight of numbers they forced us off the crest, and sent us staggering, reeling down the hill, desperate now.

Yet again Lord Stirling called on us to follow, and yet again we charged them home.

Men lay wounded, men lay dying, all across the long hillside, and more than half our number were dead or sorely stricken.

Yet it was for a fifth time that Stirling's voice rang clear, over the roar of the battle, and for the fifth time we picked up the gauge of their challenge, and swept forward in the charge.

Thus for the last time we reached the crest, and for one heroic moment held our own, and then came reeling back from the shock. And, as I was carried down the hill with the retreating line, I saw the tall figure of Lord Stirling standing upright and alone amid the storm of bullets, courting death and disdaining to retreat.

"To the rescue of Lord Stirling," I cried to the few soldiers who were around me. Dick, who was near, echoed my shout, and we dashed forward, determined to bring him off by force if no other way could be found.

But we had not advanced a dozen yards before every man that was with us had fallen and only Dick and I reached Lord Stirling, who was calmly awaiting the end.

"The day is lost, my lord," I cried, "but we have yet time to save you."

"Save yourselves, lads," he replied; "you have done everything that men can do, but it remains for me either to die or surrender."

"My lord," I cried; but at this moment Dick reeled. "Struck, by George!" he exclaimed, and I caught him as he fell.

"See to your comrade," said Lord Stirling; "you have yet time to escape."

So, throwing Dick's arms around my neck, for there was no time to parley under that rain of lead, I bore him quickly down the hill.

But our work had not been in vain, for as a soldier came to my assistance I saw that the last of the fugitives had reached the other side, and the army for the moment was saved.

And so, when we reached the banks of Gowanus Creek, we formed in line once more and gave a parting yell of defiance; then, turning, we plunged into the creek and swam to the other side, while the shot and grape from the English on the hill tore across the whole surface of the water.

Dick was badly wounded, but, with the soldier's assistance, I swam with him across the creek and bore him safely out of the range of the fire.

Ah, it was but a shadow of our former line when we formed once more, but the great General himself came to thank us, and that shadow of a line was worth a thousand men.

Thereafter we claimed as our own the post of honour in advance or in retreat; during the famous march on the night after the battle, and in the retreat to White Plains, we formed the rear guard, and the army felt secure.

There came a breathing time one day during the retreat, and the General rode up to our lines. We greeted him with the yell he loved to hear, for it brought back to him the Southland and the hunting fields of Old Virginia.

Then he told our officers that he wanted us to pick out the youngest of our line to carry a special despatch to the Committee of Public Safety, sitting at Annapolis, announcing the battle and the famous part we had taken therein. The choice fell on me, as poor Dick was groaning in the hospital, but luckily out of danger from his wound.

"Well, my boy, how old are you?" said the General, smiling down upon me, as I saluted.

"Eighteen, General."

"Do you think you can carry this safely?"

"I was in the charge at Gowanus Ford, General," said I modestly.

"I see," laughed the General, "you are a true Marylander. I wish I had more of you in the army."

CHAPTER X

THE HARRYING OF THE TORY

I was soon riding southward, the bearer of the message from General Washington to the Council of Safety, sitting at Annapolis; and as I rode, the people hailed me for my news, and gave me food and drink, so I could hurry on.

At last I reached the borders of Maryland, and again rode under the old oak from which I had torn the proclamation. It was only a few weeks before, and I wondered what had been the fate of Charles Gordon.

So, as I rode through the Head of Elk late that afternoon and came to the ferry there, I asked the boatman what they had done with him.

"Forfeiture has been decreed," he answered, "and the new High Sheriff and James Rodolph have gone today with a posse and many men to root the traitor out."

"How long ago did they start?"

"About an hour."

"What road did they take?"

"The river road. They expect to reach there about nine o'clock. Jupiter! I'd like to be there and see the flames reddening the sky. It will be a grand sight." He looked longingly through the forest toward the Braes.

"Something else will be dyed crimson, if I know that Tory right."

"That there will be, sir; it will be a lovely scrimmage;" and he sighed at the lost opportunity.

The boat grounded on the south bank, and I mounted Toby.

"A pleasant ride, sir."

"Thanks; good-night."

"Toby," said I, as I patted his neck, "you have travelled many a mile today, old fellow; but you will have to cover the ground tonight as you never covered it before. They have an hour's start, and we have a longer distance to go; so double your legs under you, my boy, and go."

Toby rising to the occasion, and the spirit of old Ranter proving true, he broke into the long even gallop that makes the miles pass swiftly. It was a race against time, against James Rodolph and his crew. I knew if once they gained the Braes, black death would stalk among the ruins, for Charles Gordon would never surrender.

The night fell rapidly as we raced along and the miles flew by.

As Toby and I drew near Bohemia Manor, where the road joined the one on which the posse was marching, I reined him in and rode more cautiously. It was well that I did so, for as I approached I heard the low murmur of men's voices and saw their figures in the dim light as they were marching by.

I brought Toby to a halt. The road was cut off that way, so I wheeled him around to ride back a short distance to where the road skirted the open fields of Bohemia Manor. As Toby plunged forward in answer to my spur, I heard a cry and then a shot came whistling by. But I left them behind, and coming to the open fields, I put Toby at the fence and raced across the open country, through the lower fields to the Braes, Toby taking the fences in his stride.

Then I dashed once more across the green lawn of the Braes and drew my sword hilt across the shutter.

There was a stir in the room above me; the shutter was cautiously opened and I was covered by the muzzle of a pistol.

"Who are you?" demanded a voice which I knew to be Charles Gordon's.

"James Frisby of Fairlee," I replied. "I have ridden to warn you, Mr. Gordon. You have only a few minutes to escape in; James Rodolph, with a hundred men behind him, will be here in ten minutes."

"Thank you, lad, for the information. I will give them a warm reception."

"But you cannot hold the Braes against a hundred men; they will burn you out, and then Mistress Jean."

"Hum; that is so, lad. Ride round to the rear of the house."

I did so, and a moment later, they came out on the little porch. The old gentleman had buckled on his sword, and there were pistols in his belt. And she, ah! she never looked more bewitching. Her beautiful hair flowed wild about her shoulders, over the light dark mantle in which she was wrapped. By the flicker of the candle, I saw that a bright flush mantled her cheek, as she spoke rapidly.

"Father, there is an English vessel a few miles down the bay. Call the slaves and escape to it."

"But I cannot take you there."

"I will carry her through the lines," I cried, "and see her safe in the hands of her aunt in Kent."

They hesitated, but the noise in front of the house told of the approaching mob, and there was no time for parley. So, true to my race, I acted quickly, and stooping from my saddle I caught her up gently and placed her on Toby before me.

"It is the only chance, lad. See that you carry her safely."

"I will carry her through or die," I replied with deep conviction. At the touch of the spur Toby sprang forward under his double burden.

"The creek," she cried.

"Yes; but we can swim it."

Indeed it was our only way, as the mob blocked the other roads of escape, so we rode boldly in and swam for the other side. The creek was several hundred yards wide, but Toby bore us bravely until we reached the southern shore, then he plunged forward, threw himself up the bank, and we were out of immediate danger.

There we halted for a moment under the shadow of a great tree and looked back across the water.

We heard the sound of many voices, the howling of the mob, and through the trunks of the trees flickered the glare of the torches. Suddenly shots rang out, a cry of dismay and rage followed, and then the flash of guns and a rattling volley crashed around the house.

"By Jove, he is fighting it out!" But the slender figure on my arm trembled, and I saw that her face was white through the darkness.

"He will escape, Mistress Jean," I said reassuringly; "trust an old Highlander for that." And I saw that her eyes were bright and tense, watching the scene across the water.

"There he goes," she exclaimed joyfully; and there, gliding swiftly through the waters, where the shadow of the trees made the darkness more intense, was a long low boat rowed by stalwart slaves. The sound of the oars was drowned by the clamour of the mob.

"If he passes the neck," I exclaimed, "he will be safe;" for the creek narrowed at its mouth until it was but a hundred yards wide.

"Ride quick to the point," she said.

So Toby plunged forward again at the pressure of my knees, and though he still went gallantly on, I could tell that the strain and the toil of the long march from the north, and his dash from the Head of Elk, were beginning to tell on him.

At last we reached the mouth of the creek, and I brought Toby to a halt under the shadow of a clump of trees, where we could see and yet not be seen. I glanced for a moment out over the waters of the bay, and I saw, several miles to the southward, the gleam of a light as it fell on the waves; I knew it was the English man-of-war.

But Mistress Jean's eyes were eagerly searching the waters of the creek, and she was straining her ears to catch the sound of the oars. Then we were rewarded. For at that moment we heard the long sweep of the oars in the water, and out from the mouth of the creek came the boat, the brawny negroes bending to their task.

The commanding figure of the old Tory stood in the stern, looking back up the creek whence they came. Unconsciously my glance followed his, and I saw that the sky was crimson, and high above the tree-tops the flames licked the skies.

"The Braes!" I exclaimed, and Mistress Jean was about to call out, when there came the sound of galloping hoofs on the other side. A horseman dashed into view, and rode into the water up to the saddle-girths. There was a flash, and the crack of a pistol broke the stillness of the night; then with a gesture of rage, the horseman rose in his stirrups and hurled the pistol far over the water; we heard the splash as it fell.

Then the figure in the boat raised his clenched hand and shook it at the horseman and the flames.

"You fired too quick, Mr. Rodolph," said the ferryman.

"Yes, damn him, he has escaped." He turned his horse and rode into the darkness, while a soft voice whispered in my ear,—

"Thank God."

CHAPTER XI

THE COUNCIL OF SAFETY

The sun had risen when we came once more in view of the groves of Fairlee. Toby's pace had degenerated into a walk, as if not to disturb the fair burden he bore, for she, overcome with fatigue and excitement, was quietly sleeping with her head on my shoulder. Toby picked his way like a dancing-master, and though the road was rough, never once did he stumble; he still bore himself gallantly for the old House of Fairlee. Ah! Toby, that road was miles too short for your master. Willingly would he have ridden thus, aye, until his hair had turned as white as snow on his brows, until the hand that guided the reins became too feeble to grasp them; aye, even unto the end of time.

But before us lay Fairlee, and beyond that lay duty and the army. "Look once more, my cavalier," said I to myself; "look once more, for the moments are short, and in the days to come, in the dreary bivouacs and on the long marches, when the world seems bare and cold, the memory of that sweet face will brighten up with sunshine your existence and make it all glorious again. Oh, hang it, here is Fairlee!"

"Mistress Jean," I whispered. I was loath to wake her, but it had to be done. "Mistress Jean!" I said, this time louder, and she awoke with a start. "This is Fairlee, and you can rest here with my mother, while I push on."

"Fairlee? Why, where am I? Oh, I remember now. Did I go to sleep, Mr. Frisby?"

"You did, Mistress Jean."

A quick, blush came.

"Oh," she said, "how can I thank you? I don't deserve——"

"Ah, Mistress Jean, it is I who do not deserve that pleasure. I would go through a hundred fights to be able to do it again; but you are tired, and I will rouse the house."

So, hammering on the door, I soon brought John Cotton to it. His woolly hair almost went straight on seeing me, and he started back, for he thought he saw my ghost.

"Good Lord, Mars Jim," he stammered, "does that be you?"

"Yes, you black scamp." And I soon convinced him of my real personality.

"But, Mars Jim, who is dat you got wid you? It ain't one of dem Yankee ladies, is it?" For, I am sorry to say, John Cotton did not approve of the ladies in question, and was afraid I would "disgrace de family" if I married one of them. Before I could answer I heard a glad little cry, and there was my mother, coming down the stairway of the great hall.

"How is my little lady?" said I, as I picked her up and kissed her, and then I introduced Mistress Jean to her and told her of our adventure at the Braes.

Then my mother went up to her, in her stately little way, and took her hands in hers, and kissed and welcomed her to the House of Fairlee.

So they made friends with each other then and there, as women do, and my mother led her away, up the broad stairs, and I stood looking after them. Then I turned to my own room, and, throwing myself on the bed, I slept the sleep of exhaustion for many hours.

When the hour of my awakening came I sprang up, for there lay the despatch which I was to bear to the Council of Safety.

Drawing on my riding-boots and buckling on my sword, I called John Cotton to bring my horse to the door, for several miles lay between Fairlee and Rock Hall, where the boat lay to take me to Annapolis.

I walked across to the hall and on to the old porch, where I saw Mistress Jean standing, gazing wistfully out on the broad bay.

"He is safe now, Mistress Jean."

"Yes," she said with a sad smile, "but when shall I ever see him again?"

"Just as soon as we whip them," I replied.

"Then it will never be," came her retort.

"Oh, ho! What will your uncle, Captain Nicholson, say when he finds he has such a fiery little Tory in his house? He will have to give up chasing the redcoats to suppress the Goddess of Sedition in his own camp."

But at this Mistress Jean gave her head a toss and walked away to the end of the porch.

Then John Cotton brought the horse to the steps.

"Are you going so soon, Mr. Frisby?"

"I must," I answered; "I am a bearer of despatches to the Council of Safety. I would gladly desert my trust to be your escort to Chestertown, but—"

"The honour of the House of Fairlee stands in the way," said she mockingly.

"Not that, my lady," I replied, bowing courteously, "but the fact that I would fall even lower in your good graces."

"Well said, cavalier," she retorted, with a sweeping courtesy. "'Tis a pity that so fine a gentleman should be a rebel."

"Or so fair a maid a Tory."

"Is this a minuet?" came the laughing voice of my mother from the door.

"Nay, mother, I am only bidding Mistress Jean good-bye with all due ceremony."

A few moments later I was in the saddle, trotting slowly off, while behind me fluttered their handkerchiefs, waving good-bye.

Rock Hall lies on a bluff, looking out across the bay. To the southward lies the Isle of Kent, with its fertile fields of waving grain, and off there on the horizon the greenish ribbon near the sky line tells where the hills of Anne Arundel lay.

Down below, under the bluff, lay a long, slender boat, shaped like a canoe, but much larger, stouter, stronger, and far swifter, when the wind filled its sails and carried it like a bird skimming over the waters.

"An English man-of-war is lying off the Isle of Kent now," said the old waterman in answer to my question, "but we can walk all around her in this boat."

"Then we will start immediately," I replied, and placing my things on board we were soon under way.

The wind caught our sails; we stood out into the bay gloriously, and she fairly flew through the water. As we rounded the Isle of Kent we saw, lying almost in our track, the English man-of-war, lazily rolling with the tide.

Then there was a great bustle on board, and the sailors flew to the rigging, the sails filled with the wind, and through the port hole was run the ugly muzzle of a Long Tom. The waterman with me laughed merrily.

"They think they can stop us," said he, but he never altered his course.

So we bore down on her until there came a flash; a cannon ball came ricochetting across the water, but fell short by a hundred yards.

The waterman chuckled. "That is about the right distance," said he; and the boat answering the helm, fairly danced around his Majesty's representative, always, by a saving grace, just beyond cannon shot.

And when his Majesty's ship actually gave chase and sent a broadside after our impertinent piece of baggage the waterman fairly danced with delight and led her a merry chase down the bay until we were opposite Annapolis. Then with a flirt of her sail we bade them good-bye and ran for the mouth of the Severn. Gaining that, we soon passed the charred hulk of the Peggy Stewart and ran up beside the wharf, and I found myself walking the streets of that gay little capital.

It was growing somewhat late, but I made my way at once to the State House, where the Convention of the Freemen of the Province sat, hoping still to find them at their deliberations. I paused for the moment when I came to the foot of the knoll on which the State House stands, for it had only recently been completed, and was the noblest building in America. Its massive proportions towered high above me, overawing the town at its feet, and commanding the country for miles around. But it was not a time for halting. Hurrying up the long flights of steps, I found myself in the great lobby, with its lofty ceilings and its air of vastness.

The Convention had adjourned but a short time before, and the lobby was still filled with men. As I threaded my way through them my dusty uniform and muddy boots marked me out as a bearer of despatches.

"News from the army—victory or defeat?" cried eager voices around me. Answer them I would not, but hurried on to the room where sat the Council of Safety, who held the fate and the fortunes of the province in its hand and was the heart and soul of the great revolt.

An usher stood at the door, but, seeing my uniform, threw it wide open, and, as I entered, softly swung it to behind me. It was a lofty room in which I found myself, with immense windows looking out over the town and the sweep of the waters of the bay to the distant line of the eastern shore. A long, broad table extended down the centre of the room. Around it were seated some sixteen or eighteen gentlemen. Staid men and grave they were, past the middle age of life, for the younger men had gone to fight the battles of the republic; men who were fitted by experience to guide the province through the stormy scenes of the civil war.

At their head sat a venerable gentleman whom I knew to be Matthew Tilghman, the patriarch of the Colony. At his right hand sat a man of sturdy build, ruddy countenance, and dark hair and eyes, more like a prosperous planter with many acres and numerous slaves than the man who was soon to become the Great War Governor of Maryland. All down the table on either side sat men with strong, determined faces, whose names bespoke the chieftainship of many a powerful family. A movement of interest ran down the table as I entered and delivered to the venerable

Chairman the despatch. He broke the seal with nervous fingers, and then rising, read General Washington's despatch aloud amid intense interest.

"Battle," "defeat," "rout," "Cortelyou House," "the Maryland Line." "Good, I see the boys did their duty," were among the many exclamations I heard around the table and when the despatch ended.

"The bearer will describe the battle."

They all turned to me, and Thomas Johnson said: "Come, young gentleman, tell us everything you saw and heard."

So I took my place by the Chairman and told them of what I had seen and done, amid many interruptions and eager questions from the Council.

Thus for a time, as I stood there, I became a man of importance, telling the tale of the battle, of the defeat and the rout, of the fiery charges, the death, the pain and the anguish of it all, until long after the night had fallen. But an end comes to all things, and Thomas Johnson, laying his hand on my shoulder, said:

"Young gentleman, you must stay with me tonight."

I accepted gladly, for the inns were crowded, and it was somewhat late in the evening to find a friend to take me in. We strolled across the State House grounds under the soft September skies, through the wide, dusty streets, until we came to the future Governor's house. Though it was late, we talked for yet another hour, and then, with a cheery good-night, I was shown to my room.

CHAPTER XII

THE VETO OF A MAID

Ah, I am afraid the clean white sheets, the soft springy bed, and the balmy September air proved traitor to me, after the hardships of a soldier's life in the field, the rough bivouac, and the hard ride from the North, for when I awoke with a start, I found the sun high in the heavens and the music of birds coming through the open window from the trees outside. Hurriedly dressing, I opened my door and went down the broad stairway into the old hall. Everything was quiet, not a soul was around. I wandered across the hall and parlour, and there I stood for a few minutes, looking out into the street, when a merry burst of laughter across the hall attracted my attention. The door of the room opposite was slightly ajar, and I saw that it was the library of the house; so crossing the hall, I gently rapped on the panel. A cheery "Come in!" was my answer. I obeyed the summons, threw the door open, and entered.

"Why, it is our feather-bed soldier," came a merry voice from the broad window-sill, where sat two young ladies. A peal of ringing laughter followed; for, indeed, I was somewhat nonplussed to thus come upon two such laughing, merry girls.

One was dark, the other fair;
Both were sweet and debonair.

Indeed they were very pretty, sitting there amid the quaint old surroundings, the heavy old book-presses, with solid oak doors, the wainscoting extending to the ceiling, the broad window-seats, the green trees, and quiet garden beyond. I knew at once that they must be daughters of my host, Mistress Polly and Mistress Betsy Johnson, at that time the reigning belles of the western shore.

"Now I know what awaited me I shall never forgive that feather-bed," I replied, recovering from my confusion and making my best bow. "I would never have proved such a traitor to my cloth."

"That is better," said Mistress Polly, the black-haired, dark-eyed one. "Come and report to us, sir. Do you not know that no officer returns from the army who does not immediately report to us?"

"I understand their alacrity in doing so. I shall be among the first to obey the order hereafter."

"Then, sir, come tell us of the battle, and what brought you hither so fast that the mud is still upon your boots?"

Now, telling the account of the battle to two charming young ladies, whose bright eyes and eager faces told of the interest they took in my narrative, was a far different thing from telling the same tale before the powerful Council of Safety, and I am free to confess that I enjoyed the last far more than the first.

Their exclamations and excited questions spurred me on, and I drew the picture of the battle with a stronger hand and painted myself a hero, which I am afraid I was far from being.

But Mistress Betsy suddenly sat up straight, exclaiming:

"Bless me, Polly, Mr. Frisby has not had his breakfast, and here it is near ten o'clock"—an outrageous late hour in those days.

At this both Mistress Polly and Mistress Betsy sprang to their feet, and I was duly conducted to the dining-room, where a delightful breakfast awaited me, which I endeavoured to eat amid their sallies and their questioning.

We were having a very gay time of it, when there came a heavy step through the hall into the room, and a cheery voice asked: "How is the soldier today? In good hands, I see." It was Thomas Johnson.

"That he is, sir," I replied, rising, "and he thoroughly enjoys it too."

"Spoken like a soldier," replied our future Governor, "and like a soldier you must leave at once, for the Council desire you to carry these despatches posthaste to General Washington."

"No; he shall not," cried Mistress Polly, with a stamp of her foot. "He has promised to drive our four-in-hand to the races this afternoon, and I am not going to let that Council of old fogies rob us of the only soldier in town who has seen service for at least one day."

"So that is the way the wind blows," said her father, pinching her cheek and laughing. "I will tell the great Council of Public Safety that they have been overruled by a maid."

"It will not be the first time," she retorted. "Their wives overrule them every day."

"I will ride all night to make it up," I suggested.

"Never mind, my boy," he replied, "you deserve a little holiday; you need not leave Annapolis until nightfall, and Kent the following night, which will give you a chance to see your mother again. There, I hope this little minx will give me some peace now."

The treaty was quickly sealed by a kiss, and Mistress Polly ran off to give the order for the coach-and-four, for the races began at one o'clock and the course was a short distance out of the city.

There soon came a clatter of hoofs, a rattle, a slam and a bang, a whoaing, a yelling, and a confusion of noises.

"They have put the colts in," cried Mistress Betsy with glee, and Mistress Polly was at the door crying, "Come on."

"Great Jove!" said I to myself, as I seized my hat and followed after, for though I had driven many a wild team I had never done so through a town before. And four devils they were for a certainty, a little under size, but making up for that by the fire and vim of their proceedings.

The heels of the wheelers were playing like castanets on the dashboard, while the leaders were in the air half the time as they swayed above the crowd of darkies, who, hanging on everywhere, were trying to hold them down, while the great coach swayed and rocked behind.

There was a flash of skirts, a gleam of the smallest feet in the world, and Mistress Polly and Mistress Betsy were in their places, and I had sprung to my seat and gathered the reins in my hands.

"All ready, Captain?"

"Ready. Let go." They scattered like chaff. There was a flash of hoofs and they were off like a shot, their bodies stretched low to the ground, the great coach rolling and rocking behind.

Luckily the street ended in a country road, for the street and the houses were gone in an instant, and we were rushing along between green fields. A column of dust rose up and whirled behind us, and the road stretched like a ribbon before, while the young ladies at my side laughed and clapped their hands in glee. After several miles the pace began to tell, I slowly brought them under control, and by the time I had come to the race-course I had them well in hand. We had gone several miles out of our way, but by taking a short cut we arrived at the races on time. I brought the four colts into the field with a dash and a flourish as they were preparing for the first race.

The course was a great level field of greensward, oval in shape, with the track in beautiful condition. Far down the track on either hand, almost encircling the field, stretched the lines of the coaches, chariots, gigs, and wagons. Gentlemen on horseback and on foot, an eager, bustling crowd, gay with colours and bright faces, already tingling with the excitement of the coming race, made a stirring scene; for the Trinity of the Marylanders in the early days of my youth were the horse, the hounds, and a fight.

But though the faces were fair, merry, and pleasant to look

upon, though the chariots and four-in-hands were gorgeous and bedecked, there was a woful lack of cavaliers to make those damask cheeks mantle with a blush, for they were away fighting in the North. Thus it was, as I drove down the line in my uniform of scarlet and buff, to find a stand, that Mistress Polly and Mistress Betsy had their triumph, and many a fair face turned our way as we drove by, until I brought the coach to a halt in a good place next to the parson, where he sat his cob, watching the preliminaries.

"Find the parson," said Mistress Polly judiciously, "and you will have found the best place in the field."

"Oh, Mistress Polly, you are a minx," said that reverend gentleman. "How in the world could I make the youngsters come to church if they did not know I was a good judge of horseflesh as well as a minister?"

"They are off," cried Mistress Betsy. The race had begun; but why describe the race? Those who have never seen a race are mere worthless creatures deserving no consideration, and those who have seen a race do not need a description. At the mere name they see the grand thoroughbreds at the line, their coats shining like satin in the sun, eager and ready to be off. Then the flag falls, and, amid the rustling of skirts and craning of necks, they are off. Ah, and then comes the glorious excitement of it all as you watch with eager eyes that ribbon of a track, and see now this one, now that one, slowly draw away from the bunch at the start, and the closing of the space again, until they become mere moving spots on the far side of the field. And then, that home stretch, with its thunder of hoofs, its roar of voices, and cheers and yells, as the grand beasts, with straining nerves and neck to neck, make the last great effort; and afterward the triumph, the waving of handkerchiefs, the great cheer that greets the victor, and the smiles of merry lips and laughing eyes. Those were the prizes we raced for, when racing was the pastime of gentlemen, and not an excuse for blackguardism and gambling, as today it is fast becoming. So my kind hosts and I made our little bets, and enjoyed ourselves right thoroughly, until the last race, which was won by a grandson of the great Selim, was over and done. Then I swung my four colts into the road again, and at a rattling pace returned to town.

It was late now, and the sun was preparing to take its last dip behind the western hills; so I was forced to bid my charming hostesses adieu, and amid many good wishes and a waving of handkerchiefs, departed to seek my waterman, to begin my trip across the bay.

The town became a blur, a dark mass behind us, broken by the twinkling of the lights through the gloom, as we swiftly glided down the Severn before the wind. Out upon the bay it was still light, and we steered for the north point of the Isle of Kent. The wind was fresh. With all sail set we skimmed the water before it, and ere many hours had passed we saw the light through the gloom of Rock Hall straight ahead. But the old waterman suddenly brought his helm around hard, and pointed her nose for the wide mouth of the Chester close at hand.

"What is wrong?" I asked, and for an answer he pointed with his arm to where against the sky were outlined the tapering masts of a large vessel lying between us and Rock Hall.

"That is a man-of-war," he said, "we will have to run up the river to Chestertown."

"Agreed," said I, right readily, for I thought I might see Mistress Jean once more before I went back to the front.

The mouth of the Chester was soon gained, and for hours, through the stillness of the night, we glided over its smooth waters, between low, heavily wooded banks, or the broad sweeping fields of some plantation, whose boundaries were lapped by the waters of the river. In the early morning, in the dusky gray hours, we ran along beside the wharf of the old county seat of Kent.

CHAPTER XIII

THE GREETING OF FAIR LIPS

After wandering through the streets of this old town during the early hours of the morning, seeing it gradually wake into life and take on the quiet bustle of the day, I at last found myself before the inn, which had just been opened.

The host was an old friend, and we were soon fighting over the battles again, when a shadow fell across us and I sprang to my feet.

It was Capt. James Nicholson, one of the three brothers who fought their ships in sunshine and in storm, while there was a plank left for them to stand upon, carrying dismay through the English fleets by their desperate courage and daring. He was a man about forty years old, over medium height, but slender and of fair complexion, with light blue eyes and reddish hair, a typical descendant of that old Viking, Nicholson, who fought some famous fights under King Haco, and harried the coasts of Scotland until he gained a foothold there and founded the Scottish family of the name. The same open, bold countenance of the Admiral, the same frank and manly bearing, showed him to be a sailor and a fighter.

"Hello, Frisby," said he, shaking my hand cordially. "With the dove so near I knew that the hawk would not be far away."

I stammered out, as the landlord smiled, that I was forced to come to Chestertown to avoid the man-of-war lying off Rock Hall.

"She is off Rock Hall, is she? Well, I shall have to chase her away with the Defence next week. But is that your only excuse for coming so far out of your way?"

And when I protested that it was, he laughed genially, and, turning to the landlord, said: "He does not look like a knight-errant who flies to the rescue of maids, and Tory maids at that, does he? But see here, youngster, since you have brought this little traitress into my household, you will have to do your share in converting her to the true principles of liberty and democracy."

"Keep that for the men, Captain," cried the landlord. "Keep that for the men; the women give us no peace, as it is, and if they once get those notions there will be no living with them."

"Ah, you old reprobate, you had better not let your wife hear you."

With this we left the inn, and going through some quiet streets, we at last came to Water Street, with its square brick houses, gardens and flowers, and green lawns leading to the river. Very substantial were the buildings, quaint and old-fashioned. A number of white steps led from the street to the porch of the Captain's house. When, at his motion, I opened the door and stepped into the hall, which was somewhat dark after the glare of the street, there came a flurry of lace, and soft arms were around my neck. And—well, what could a man do but return that kiss with interest? But the best things are but fleeting, for, when she glanced at my face, and saw who I was, she gave a little cry, broke from my arms, and vanished in confusion up the stairway, followed by the merry laughter of the real uncle, not the proxy.

"You surely cannot object to that welcome, Frisby; but I must tell Mistress Jean to be more careful, or the army will lose a promising officer. They will not be able to keep you away from the town if this keeps on."

So saying, he led the way to the rear porch where it overlooked the lawn and the river.

Here we sat and talked until the breakfast-bell rang, and we went into the dining-room. I was as hungry as a trooper by this time, after my all-night experience on the Chester.

The dining-room was a long room, with open windows looking out across the river and the fields.

We had not as yet taken our seats, when through another door came Mistress Jean and Mistress Nancy Nicholson, her bosom friend and confidante, with their arms around each other's waists—a charming picture.

The colour mantled high on Mistress Jean's cheek, and I am sure that mine played the traitor also, but Mistress Nancy came to the rescue by demanding news and particulars of her cavalier, for such she declared Mr. Richard Ringgold of Hunting Field to be.

Answering, I told her that I had left him covered with blood and with glory, but on the fair road to recovery. And so, though Mistress Jean still showed a heightened colour, in telling of Master Richard's fortunes and escapes we broke the embarrassment of the meeting, and were soon fast friends again. It was a merry breakfast. Afterward the two young ladies and I walked in the garden by the river's edge and talked of many things,—of war and campaigning, for I claimed to be an authority by now, and quite a veteran,—of love; but that was too dangerous, for Mistress Nancy would look at me slyly and laugh as she asked if I was as great an authority upon the one as I was upon the other.

I retorted that I had heard many a lecture on the subject from Master Richard, but otherwise knew nothing of the art, and then I begged her to take me as a pupil, so that in time I might become as great a scholar as Dick himself. But she roguishly recommended me to her Assistant Professor Mistress Jean Gordon, who, she told me, knew more of the art than she did herself. And then, having come to some boxwood alleys, she slipped away and left Mistress Jean and me alone.

"They tell me, Mistress Jean, that love is war; may I ask what the fate of the prisoners is?"

"As in real war," she replied, "those who surrender at discretion receive but scant courtesy, but those who make a gallant resistance are often victorious in their defeat."

"I see that you love the old Highland fashion, where the bridegroom came with force and arms and bore the bride away."

"Better swords and daggers, and hearts that are true, than silks and satins, Lowland fops and perfidy."

"English swords have crossed ere this with Highland steel, and English hearts are as tried and as true as those that beat beneath the plaid," said I, coming to the defence of my English ancestry.

"So ho! Sir Rebel!" she cried in glee, "what means this defence of the hated redcoat? Do you not fear the shadow of the great committee that you preach treason so openly?" And she looked so bewitching in her little triumph that I had to thrust my hands into my pockets and turn away, so great was the temptation.

"I will turn Highlander," said I, "if you do not stop."

"Stop?" she said with the most innocent air in the world.

"Aye," said I, "for if your Highlanders have ever been sturdy knaves, the Frisbys have ever been quick where bright eyes and ruby lips are concerned, and there is no telling what might happen." And I looked so determined and fierce that she broke into merry laughter in my face.

"Your fate be upon you," said I solemnly; and—well, at that moment, I heard Captain Nicholson calling that my horse was at the door, waiting for me.

"That means that I must go, Mistress Jean," and the laughter died on her lips, "go to join my comrades in the North in their struggle for the Great Cause. When you hear of battles and sieges and sudden deaths, will you sometimes think of the young rebel who rode with you from the Braes to Fairlee? For wherever he may be, whether in the glory of the rush and the sweep of the charge, or the gloomy and dismal retreat; whether in the camp on the bleak hillside, with the cold north wind blowing, or bivouacked in the Southern savannahs warmed by the rays of the sun; in the fatigue and the toil of the marches, amid the groans and cries of the dying, or the joy and triumph of the hour when the fight has been fought and won, your smile shall always be with him, the light of your eye in his heart. Will you think of him, or forget, Mistress Jean?"

"I will think of him." Her voice was very low and sweet. Then I stooped and kissed her hand, the fairest hand that man ever looked upon.

CHAPTER XIV

THE RETURN OF THE TORY

As I turned to ride away, after bidding good-bye to the Captain, I heard a voice calling me, and looking up, I saw Mistress Nancy at a window, and riding under it she commanded me to convey to Master Richard a tiny case wrapped in many papers.

"And now, sir," said she, "here is something for you;" and she threw me a little case, which, on opening quickly, I saw contained a miniature of a fair young girl, with a wealth of dark brown hair, the loveliest eyes and the sweetest face.

"Mistress Nancy," I cried, "you are my guardian angel." Placing the miniature over my heart, I threw her a kiss, and rode on my way rejoicing.

I rode from Chestertown to Fairlee, where I bade my mother good-bye, and from there I took up the trail to the North, riding into camp one evening just as the sun was setting.

I reported immediately to the great General, who thanked me for the speed with which I had carried the despatches and returned. And then I was once more among my old comrades of the Line.

They crowded around me, one and all, for I had messages for many of them, and they were eager for the news of old Kent and the shore, and my welcome was right royal.

And now, for a month or so, disasters came crowding upon our arms; defeat and death stalked through our ranks, and cast a gloom over the cause.

We fought the fight at White Plains, and when Fort Washington fell many of our Maryland boys went to the hulks of old Jersey to find a last resting-place under the cold gray waters of Wallabout Bay. Amid constant marching, skirmishes, and defeats the months slipped away, and the cold gloomy winter was upon us. Ah, how cold and bleak and barren the hillsides looked after the smiling fields of Maryland, touched and warmed by the Southern sun! And then the cold, the bitter cold of it all, the white winding sheet of the snow and the ice made us shiver and hug the fire of dry fence-rails and button our threadbare coats more tightly around us, while we looked in despair at the toes peeping through the ends of our boots. But the great General knew how to warm the blood in our veins and drive the despair from our hearts, when on that bitterly cold Christmas night he led us across the Delaware and hurled us against the Hessians.

It is true that we left a trail of blood as we marched, dyeing the snow with its crimson. Yet the fight itself was glorious, and when we came back in our triumph the cold and the snow were as nothing. We made sport of our rags and tatters and laughed the English to scorn.

Then again when we struck them at Princeton seven days later, threw the dust in Cornwallis's eyes, and played with him as we willed, we were ready to follow our leader wherever he pointed the way.

And so, after humbling the English, we returned to our camp for the winter, and there made ready for the spring, when we saw my Lord Cornwallis back on the Hudson again.

Then we lay in Jersey, watching them over in New York, until far into the summer, ready to take up the march when the news should come of the destination of the English fleet that lay off Sandy Hook.

At last one day there came a horseman spurring fast from the southward, bearing the news of a vast fleet that covered the waves of the Chesapeake and lay at that moment off the harbor of Baltimore, threatening it with fire and sword.

Then there was a mighty bustle in the camp, and we whose homes were now in danger took up the march to the southward, eager to meet the foe.

When we reached Philadelphia we found that the enemy had entered the Elk, and was now marching on the city, while the hastily called Maryland and Delaware volunteers threw themselves in the way, cutting off straggling parties and obstructing the advance.

So we hurried on to assist them, and found ourselves on the evening of the 10th of September at the Brandywine, with the English advance but a few miles away.

It was here that I met with one of the volunteers, who on hearing the English were in the Chesapeake had taken his rifle from the rack and joined in the defence. He came from lower Kent, but told me of the devastation all through the county of Cecil, wherever the enemy had laid its blighting hand.

"They tell me," he said, "that the old Tory, Charles Gordon, whom they ran out of Cecil, is with Lord Howe, and high in his counsels. When they arrived in the Elk, Gordon, with a body of troops, marched all night and attacked the house of James Rodolph at dawn. Rodolph was away from home, and that is the only thing that saved him, for they say that Gordon swore that he would hang him if he once caught him. As it was, he gave Rodolph's house to the flames, and burned everything on the place. 'An eye for an eye,' said he, 'is a Highland saying as well as a Jewish one. I regret that I cannot destroy the land as well.' Rodolph, when he heard of it, stormed and swore, but he has not dared to venture within the confines of Cecil since."

"Did Gordon do anything else?" I asked.

"No. After he burnt Rodolph out he tried to stop Lord Howe from pillaging, but his lordship answered, 'You have had your turn, and now you must let the others have theirs,' and so the pillaging went on."

But the planters and the yeomen who had risen at the first alarm hung on the flanks of Lord Howe's army, cutting off stragglers and scouting-parties, and confining the belt of desolation within narrow lines.

At last came the 11th of September, the day when we met Lord Howe at the Brandywine, and were sent reeling back in disorderly retreat, when by a skilful march they outflanked our right wing and rolled it up.

And then disaster followed disaster. Paoli came, that grim and bloody surprise at the dead of night. We had marched with Wayne and gained the rear of the British column, and lay for the night in a dense wood, waiting for the recruits under Smallwood, who was marching to join us, before we began our attack on the British rear.

It was in the early hours of the morning, the blackest of the night, the hour before the dawn, when there came sudden shots from our pickets, and before we could spring to arms the Highland war-cry rang through the forest and the Black Watch swept over us. The wild forms of the Highlanders, the intense darkness, the surprise, the din and noise of the strife as those who could grasp their muskets made a desperate stand, struck terror through the camp, and ere the men could rally we were swept into the woods beyond. It seemed to me, as I was borne along in the press, I heard, high over the charging cry of the Scots, the voice of the old Tory cheering his men on. Certain it is that I saw him for a moment by the light of a camp-fire, sword in hand, urging on his wild Scots, who seemed to grow wilder under his leadership, as our line melted away before their advance.

Ah! but it was grim and terrible. Our men, overcome by the surprise and the rout, carried terror into the camp of Smallwood's recruits, which was near at hand, and they, too, gave way.

But the dawn came: with it we gathered our shattered forces

together and marched back to join Washington.

Philadelphia fell, but the tide soon turned; for at German-town we once more met them and avenged the surprise at Paoli.

But the thing that thrilled us through and through and set our banners high was the courage of our brothers of the Line, who, thrown into Fort Mifflin, held it in the teeth of the enemy's fire until every gun was dismounted and the fort itself levelled to the earth, leaving nothing to defend. It was a brave and gallant action, and we envied them for their good fortune.

We had avenged Paoli at Germantown, yet this added another wreath to our banner. It was a thing to stir the blood and to set the pulses bounding to hear how those heroes fought under the crumbling walls of Mifflin, and prayed for the friendly cover of night to fall to hide them from that storm of fire and shell, and yet fought on.

CHAPTER XV

THE FLAG OF TRUCE

The long hard winter soon came on, and we retired to Valley Forge to suffer and to bear what was far more deadly than the English bullets—the terrible cold and desolation of that dreary place. Cold, bitterly cold it was, as the wind came down from the mountains, swept over the broad fields, pierced through our torn and tattered garments, and racked our frames with pain. And yet, terrible as the exposure was, there stands out one bright day in all that dreary winter, one day, one hour in which I forgot all the cold and the hardships and would not have been elsewhere for anything in the wide world.

It was near the setting of the sun on one of the bleakest and coldest days of the year. The sun itself was sinking behind the distant hills, and the sky was brilliant with its fiery javelins, which threw a lurid light across the cold gray heavens, the last protest of departing day against the approach of the chill dismal night. The snow lay heavy upon the ground, and spread like a great white pall over the sins and sorrows of the world. Before us stretched the road, unbroken and trackless; not a man had passed that way, for we stood guard at the outpost, and the flicker of the foeman's fire could be seen six hundred yards away, through the gloom.

"Lucifer, but it is cold!" said one of the guard, as he threw another rail on the fire and held his hands out over the flames to warm them.

"Aye; Old Nick himself would not be a bad acquaintance now—his smell of brimstone and sulphur might warm us up a bit," said another.

We were making the best we could of it, under the lee of a high bank by the side of the road, where we had cleared a space and stacked a good supply of dry fence-rails to feed the fire during the night. The wind from the northwest swept over our heads, sheltered as we were by the bank, and we would have defied the cold that crept ever upward but for the rags and tatters that covered our frames. The men themselves were cheerful, as they sat hugging the fire, and laughed and joked at their hardships.

"I wonder if those Highland devils will bother us tonight?" asked one, for the Black Watch held the outpost down the road.

"They will be too busy warming their knees," came the reply from across the fire, and a laugh followed.

"Hello, what is that?" for the thud of hoofs was heard on the road coming from the camp.

"A flag of truce, by George!" said the sergeant. "Who on earth wants to go through the lines on a night like this?"

The party, consisting of several troopers, an officer, and what appeared to be a woman on horseback, was soon within hailing distance, and I heard Ringgold's voice call out:

"I say, Frisby, are you in charge here?"

"Yes," I replied. "What's up?"

"We have a prisoner here who wishes to go through the lines, but I don't know whether you will permit her or not."

"Is she fair?" I asked. "For in that case she shall not pass unless she gives us a smile by way of tribute as she rides by."

"Not even if George Washington so orders, sir," said a voice that I knew.

"By the saints, my lady!" I cried, and I was by her side in an instant. "What brings you here, and why are you going within the English lines?"

"Should not a daughter be with her father?" she asked.

"But those bloody English, with all their fine trappings and their feathers! Nay, my lady, you have been disrespectful to the Continental Congress, as I can vouch for. You are our prisoner, and I will not let you escape thus, to smile on the wearers of his Majesty's uniform."

But she laughed quite merrily, and answered my threat with "Lieutenant Ringgold, pray ride on with the flag of truce."

"Dick Ringgold," I cried in my turn, "if you take less than ten minutes I shall be your deadly enemy for life."

"All right, old fellow." Dick rode on toward the enemy's campfire with the bugler until he had gone about half the way, and then we heard the parley sounded and saw a stir in the opposite camp.

"Mistress Jean," said I, returning to the charge, "you are perfectly heartless, and though I know the redcoats cannot help but fall in love with you, I warn you that if you smile on any one of them I shall go through the lines and seek him out, even into the heart of the city itself, though I have to swing for it."

"You will never try anything so rash;" and now the laughter had gone from her voice.

"That I will, my lady," I replied, "for I would rather dance on nothing than know that you belonged to another."

"But you must not," said she. "You must not think of such a thing. You must promise me never to attempt it."

"Nay, Mistress Jean, that I cannot promise. It would drive me mad to stand here on guard all the winter night and see the lights of Philadelphia off there in the east; to know amid all the gayety and the balls you reign supreme; to know I could not see you because of the miserable redcoats that guard the city. If they were ten times their number I would find my way through them to be once more at your side, Mistress Jean."

Before she could reply the Highland officer broke in, for he had ridden up with Ringgold.

"Mistress Jean, it gives me pleasure to be the first to welcome you to our lines. Your father told us of your coming, and there has been a rivalry between us as to who should be the one to escort you to the city."

"That was kind of all of you; but how did you leave my father?"

"Well, and eager for your coming."

He was a splendid-looking young fellow, tall, broad-shouldered, and somewhat bony, with a voice that rang frank and true. He was a Highlander, every inch of him, and carried himself with a free and graceful carriage, and when I heard him tell Mistress Jean that he was a Farquharson and an old ally of her house, I knew I had at last met a dangerous rival. For, out of romances, it is not the villain, but the brave and frank gentleman who is most dangerous to the peace of mind of lovers, for they see in him what they themselves most admire, and by which they hope to win their ladies' love.

"Lieutenant Ringgold, now," said Farquharson, "I am ready to receive Mistress Gordon from your hands, and to conduct her within our lines."

"Far more ready than we are to let her go," answered Dick gallantly; "but it is the fortune of war." And then the two officers saluted and the exchange was made.

So Mistress Jean bade us all good-bye right prettily, and I, being on the off side of her horse from the others, seized her hand as it hung by her side and kissed it several times. She at first did not withdraw it, and then, bending over, whispered, "Do not try to enter the city, for they will hang thee, and I would not lose so true a friend." Here her voice was very soft and low. I kissed her hand once again and she was gone.

We watched their dark shadows down the road to the Highland outpost, as they moved like great blots across the snow. I stood, I do not know how long, gazing after them, when Dick's hand was on my shoulder.

"Never mind, Frisby," said he, "we shall win the city in the spring, and then you may win her also."

CHAPTER XVI

THE BALL OF MY LORD HOWE

Many a night after that last parting I stood guard on that dreary outpost, gazing out across the snow at the dim lights of the city far to the eastward. Aye, for the city was gay that winter, gay with parties and dances, balls and dinners, and the bells rang as merrily as if we were not starving and dying out on the bleak, hillsides. Aye, those old burghers were warm and comfortable as they sat by their fires, with a glass of their wine or toddy at their side.

True, my Lord Howe ruled the city with an iron hand, but he was a gallant gentleman, and his officers made good partners for their fair daughters at the balls. They were handsome in their scarlet uniforms, with their epaulets and their sabres, making, indeed, a very gallant show, while those ragged patriots out upon the snow had not shoes to their feet, and were altogether too disreputable to be admitted even to the kitchens of their houses. Then, again, runs not the Quaker law, "Thou shalt not fight"? And so the good old burghers threw another log on the fire and sat down to enjoy the cheerful blaze.

The news came to us, sifted through the lines; we heard of their dances and their balls, and everywhere we heard that Mistress Jean Gordon was the belle of them all. The old Tory held high rank in the counsels of Lord Howe, and the daughter, by her grace and beauty, reigned it over the hearts of every gallant gentleman of his army.

We heard of her refusing my Lord Paulet and several other gentlemen, noted among us for their hard fighting, whenever by chance we were opposed to them. And I, standing guard on the outpost, chafed in vain when I heard these tales, until one day chance decided me to risk all, to see her once more with my own eyes, and perhaps speak to her.

There had been a skirmish on the outposts that day, and our men had captured an English officer, a Captain of the line. He was a talkative man, and while he was waiting to be sent to the rear as a prisoner we entertained him at our mess table, and he in turn told us the news of the town.

"That must be a wonderful country, what do you call it, that eastern shore of yours?" said he, "if it contains any more beauties like Mistress Jean Gordon."

"Ah, the Tory's daughter?"

"Yes. She is the reigning belle of the whole town, and all our fellows are wild about her. I never saw so many fellows in love with one girl before, but Farquharson seems to have the best of it, while Lord Paulet stamps and swears."

Now, we were loyal Marylanders—loyal, at least, to her wit and beauty, so then and there we proposed and drank the health of the Tory maid, while Dick chimed in with the amendment, "May she never marry a Britisher, but a patriot tried and true," at which our English Captain good-naturedly protested; and while they drank the toast I made a vow that ere a week was past I would be within that city.

Fortune came my way, for as I left the mess-room that night I ran against Tom Jones of Cresap's old company of riflemen from the mountains of the West, the most daring and desperate spy in all our army. He was a man of powerful strength, as lithe and active as a panther, while his face was as immovable as that of an Indian, with never a sign thereon of the thoughts and passions of the man within. He was clad for the moment in the dress of the riflemen, a full suit of buckskin, leggings, hunting-shirt, and all, while carelessly thrown across one arm was his rifle, and in his belt was sheathed the long hunting-knife.

"Lieutenant," said he, "I expect to return through your lines tomorrow night, so do not fire before you challenge."

"Come this way, Jones," said I, leading him aside from the others. "I do not know which way you are going, but I want you to help me through the lines into the city. Can you do so?"

"But, Lieutenant, they will be wanting to hang you if you are caught."

"I will take that risk. I must be in the city within a week."

Jones, like most great frontiersmen, was a man of quick decision and few words.

"Meet me in an hour," said he, "at the Yellow Tavern."

An hour later found me at the tavern in full uniform, for it was the only suit I possessed in which it would be possible to present myself before a lady, so dilapidated, torn, and ragged was my wardrobe. But I had a great storm-coat which hid the uniform and was an admirable disguise.

The tavern was crowded. As I stood by the fire I did not at once notice a quiet, unassuming traveller who had just entered, until he brushed past my arm and whispered, "Follow me." I did so a few minutes later, for it was Tom Jones, who looked for all the world as if he was a quiet city merchant, born and bred within its limits. Yet you had but to notice his walk, and you saw at once that he was a mountaineer, for he threaded his way through the crowd as noiselessly as he did among his native forests, where the crack of a dead twig might mean his death by a hostile bullet.

I followed him out into the night, and a dark and dismal night it was; the snow was falling heavily and you could not see three rods away.

"We will follow the pike," said he, "until we see their camp-fire. They will not keep strict watch tonight, and we will have to keep in touch with the landmarks."

We trudged along through the snow past the outpost where I had commanded so many nights, keeping the vigils by the weary hours; then we became more careful, as the Highland outpost was but a few yards away.

"They will have their backs to the storm," said the spy, "and though it is dangerous to go to the windward of a foe, yet he is not so apt to hear us as he would be to see us if we tried the leeward side. Those Highlanders have keen eyes."

So we flanked the outpost to the windward and passed them safely, and then Jones led me by many little bypaths and lanes until we came to the outskirts of the town. And though the guard at one time could have touched us as they passed, so dense was the storm that never for a moment was our safety jeoparded.

At last the houses became closer and we found ourselves in the town, while every now and then a belated traveller met us, glanced our way and passed on, for by now it was far into the night. But when we reached the heart of the town, even at that hour, the streets became filled with carriages, and we met many officers and gentlemen, returning from a ball. My Lord Howe entertained that night, and it was a sign of loyalty and good faith for every one to attend.

Though I became interested in seeing the muffled figures pass us, and the carriages hurrying through the street, I grew uneasy as I saw that Jones was making his way to the centre of the town, to the very door of Lord Howe's mansion. At last I remonstrated with him, but Jones growled in answer: "How can you throw the dogs off your track, if the snow does not fill it, but by mixing it with other tracks?"

This was unanswerable. I followed him along the street until we were among the crowd before Lord Howe's door.

It was a gay and brilliant scene, that ball of my Lord Howe, and though it was near the end, the music of the dance still floated through the wide entrance, while the figures of the dancers flitted across the windows, which were ablaze with lights. The guests were fast leaving; fair ladies and officers bravely uniformed were coming down the steps. There was a calling of carriages and of names, the slamming of doors and the muffled roll of the wheels as they drove off. I was about to move on with Jones, when I heard the major-domo, a sergeant of the guard, call out the carriage of Colonel Charles Gordon, and then I would have drawn back, as I had been forced into the front rank; for, though I knew that she must be at the ball, I had not thought to be brought so suddenly face to face with her. But ere I could do so, she came down the carpeted stairs leaning on her father's arm, graceful and beautiful, while by her side walked Farquharson in full Highland costume, eager and attentive. A smile was upon her lips as she listened, and then her eyes met mine. Her face went pale, and she was near fainting. Her father caught her as she slightly reeled, and Farquharson looked fiercely around to see what the cause was. But I was muffled up, and before he could demand the cause Mistress Jean was eagerly declaring that it was a mere nothing; and, as if to prove what she said was true, she hurried on to the carriage.

Farquharson leaned for a moment into the carriage to bid them good-night, and then it rolled off into the darkness.

CHAPTER XVII

AN EXCHANGE OF COURTESIES

"A narrow escape that for you, Lieutenant," said Jones. "But she was a plucky lass, and now it is time for us to be looking for cover."

He turned down a narrow, quiet street until we came to a house set somewhat back in the yard.

Jones now rapped very gently on the door; it swung open as if he was expected, and a moment later we found ourselves heartily welcomed by an old Quaker lady in a little room with a bright fire burning.

"I thought thee would come, Brother Jones," said she, "and who is this braw lad thou hast brought with thee?" And she smiled on me.

"He is one of our Lieutenants, who has a sweetheart in town, and is willing to risk his neck to see her," said Jones gruffly, but there was a twinkle in his eye.

This completed my conquest, and the motherly old soul proceeded to take charge of me.

"Who is thy lady love thou hast come to see?" And when I told her that she was a Tory she was much distressed, but eager to help me.

"The Good Book says thou must not fight, but it also says thou must help thy friends and neighbours, so I will help thee."

But at last, after chattering awhile she took a candle and showed us to our rooms. I was soon lost in the almost blissful comfort of clean white sheets and a feather-bed.

When I awoke next morning Jones had already departed on his mission, leaving me a note telling me where to meet him the next night on our return to camp.

All that day I kept close to the house, for I did not dare to venture forth in the broad day, as I was known to many, and it would not have gone well with me if I had met with those I knew.

But at last the night began to fall, and, bidding my kind hostess good-bye, I made my way through the streets to the Tory's house.

I soon found it—a square brick structure in a quiet street. I noticed, as I approached it, several dark alleys just at the right places for a rapid retreat if the worse should come to the worst.

Then my hand was on the knocker, and its fall startled me as the clatter echoed far down the street and seemed to wake the very dead.

A slave opened the door, who, though he glanced at me suspiciously, told me that his mistress was at home.

Then in a moment my storm-coat was off, and I stood in the door of the drawing-room.

It was a beautiful picture, the great strong Highlander on his knees at the feet of Mistress Jean begging for her hand, which she seemed to be denying him, for he was growing more and more passionate.

For a moment, as I stood there, I could feel my hair grow gray, but the tumult and the conflict within me were short and I turned to go, for it seemed to me that she could not but care for so gallant a gentleman.

But her eyes met mine, and then for a moment there was terror in them, and a cry broke forth from her lips.

Farquharson, startled by her gaze, turned also, and, seeing me, was quickly on his feet, his face aflame with passion.

"Sir," said he, advancing toward me, "do you not know the fate of eavesdroppers"—and then for the first time noticing my uniform, added, "and spies?"

"I know the fate of those who call a gentleman by such names," I retorted coolly.

"A gentleman?" and he laughed. "I will have you hanged for a dog of a spy before sunrise."

"Pardon me, sir, but you are my prisoner until it shall suit me to let you go free."

At this he laughed merrily.

"Well said, Sir Rebel," he cried; "but permit me to pass before I spit you on my sword." And he drew and advanced upon me.

"Permit me, sir, to use another argument;" and I drew my pistol and covered him. "Advance another step and I will blow your brains out."

He glanced at me for a moment, but did not advance. "And further, let me suggest that we are in the presence of a lady, and it is not seemly for her to see the flash of weapons."

At this he put up his sword.

"To whom do I owe a lesson in gallantry?" he asked with a low and sweeping bow.

"James Frisby, of Fairlee, a Lieutenant in the Maryland Line," I replied with equal courtesy.

Mistress Jean had stood as though she were turned to stone during our exchange of courtesies, but now she seemed to recover.

"Captain Farquharson," she cried, and she came and stood between us, "this is an old friend of mine. He saved my life at the Braes when we were raided by the rebels. You must promise me to let him go free out of the city."

"Your wishes, Mistress Jean, are law," said he, "and shall be obeyed. I shall give him till morning to escape in."

"Which I promptly accept," said I, "with the hope that I may be able to repay your courtesy if fortune should bring you within our lines some day."

And so he bade Mistress Jean farewell, but as he passed me, I whispered to him:

"Sir, some words have been said that need an explanation."

"It will give me pleasure to offer you one at any place you may appoint."

"Then meet me," I said, "two days hence at sunrise on the pike, half-way between the lines."

"With swords or pistols?"

"Swords."

"I will be there;" and he passed on out.

When he had gone, I turned to Mistress Jean, who urged me to leave at once.

"You must go," said she, "for at any moment you may be tracked and discovered, and then——"

"And then—what?" I answered, smiling. "Do you think, Mistress Jean, that I, who travelled for miles through the snow and the storm last night to catch one glimpse of your face, that I, who at last stand in your presence, would give a thought to the noose around my neck?"

But she would not let me say her nay, and then her terror grew, until at last she told me that Lord Howe sometimes came home with her father at nine o'clock to talk over the plans of the spring campaign, and that every moment she expected to hear their voices in the hall.

"The sight of your face, Mistress Jean, has repaid me for my journey; but if you bid me go, why, then, it is fate, and go I must." Then a thought came to me. "Mistress Jean, tell me this before I leave in the enemy's camp all that is dearest on earth to me: tell me if you love that Highlander, if you care for him." And she, who a moment before was urging me to leave, stood silent, with her face turned away from me, with never a word to say.

And I, seeing how matters stood, took my courage in my hands, and, with a low bow, wished her good-bye.

CHAPTER XVIII

THE CROSSING OF SWORDS

Sunrise, two days later, found Mr. Richard Ringgold and myself stamping our feet in the snow on the pike, half-way between the hostile lines.

"I suppose they will let us fight here without interruption," said Dick.

"No danger from that," I replied. "We will fight in that little hollow, where the outposts cannot see us."

"Here they come," said Dick. We saw two officers approaching across the snow from the Highland outpost.

They soon came up, and we saluted, while Dick and Captain Forbes, Farquharson's second, soon agreed upon the preliminaries.

"Will you lead the way, gentlemen?" said Forbes.

Dick and I led them to the little hollow between the hills, where a slight meadow formed a platform, as it were, for us to act our drama upon.

Since my first duel with Rodolph on the banks of the Elk I had seen something of war and of battles, and considered myself an old hand in such encounters.

And so I found myself looking Farquharson over and estimating his strength and his skill, for I knew him to be one of the best swordsmen among the Highlanders, while I could claim, with all due modesty, to be the best in the Maryland Line.

He was a notable swordsman, you could see that at a glance; the powerful figure, yet as light and active as a cat, the muscles of his sword arm telling of long and patient handling of the weapon, while his cold gray eye spoke for his coolness and determination.

He glanced at me, as we threw off our coats, in almost an indifferent manner, as if he had a duty to perform, which was to be done as quickly as possible, the mere suppression of a country bumpkin by a gentleman of fashion. I knew that would change as soon as our swords crossed, and smiled to myself. Then, being stripped to our shirts, we took our places and saluted.

Click, and our swords rang true. Though he fenced somewhat carelessly at first, there came a surprised look and a sudden change in his manner, as I parried a skilful thrust and touched him lightly on the shoulder. He seemed to realise that he had no ordinary swordsman opposed to him, and quickly brought into play all his skill and fierceness in attack, throwing me on the defensive and forcing me gradually back.

It could not last; no strength could stand it. When he found that the steel guard met every attack, that every thrust was parried, he relaxed the fierceness of his attack and began to fence with more skill and caution.

Thus it was we fenced for several minutes, the clash of the steel ringing out in the cold, crisp air across the snow, and it came to my opponent that he had at last met a swordsman who was his equal in skill. From this on every moment he developed some new feint, some new attack, and, though I met them every one, it took my utmost skill to do so.

But at last there came the end. He had assumed the offensive again and was pressing hard upon me, when he placed his foot upon a loose stone in the snow, which rolled. The sword flew from out his hand and he was down upon his knee.

My sword was at his throat, and then my hand was stayed, for there came before me the vision of the Tory maid, standing with face averted in the square brick house in the city. That she might care, that she might be in terror then as to the fate that might befall him, flashed through my brain. I brought my sword to a salute, and returned it to its scabbard.

"Sir," said I, as Farquharson rose, "it is a pleasure to have fought with so gallant a gentleman."

"And I, sir," he returned, "am happy to have met so skilful a swordsman." And then, like gallant men who have fought and know each other's worth, we shook hands on the spot where a moment before our blades were thirsting for each other's blood.

"It gives me pleasure," he continued, "to withdraw my remarks at Colonel Gordon's, as they arose from a misapprehension."

"I will consider them as if they had never been said," I replied, "and I beg of you, on your return, to present my compliments to Mistress Gordon, and tell her that I send you to her as my wedding gift."

"Why, is she to be married?" he asked in a startled way.

"I believe so," I answered, "but she will tell you all about it."

And so we returned to the pike, where we all saluted again, and retraced our steps to the lines.

The spring was late that year. April had come before there came a soft warm breeze from the Southland, waking nature into life, and covering the hard frozen face of mother earth with wreaths and clouds of mist and moisture. From every hillside, from every frost-bound plain, the smoke of spring arose, and through the air there breathed the spirit of the reincarnated life of the world.

How we of the Southland hailed it with joy, and drank in with our lungs this promise of a new life! We who loved the sunshine and the balmy breezes, the great joy of living amid fragrant fields and green-clad forests, we who hated the storms, the wind and cold of the North,—ah, how the blood in our veins welcomed this soft caress of the South! We threw off the terror of the winter, looked forward with glee to the opening of the spring campaign, and counted in anticipation the honours we were to win, the glory that would be ours.

New life sprang up all through the camp; the troops left the busy duty of hugging the fires, the ranks filled up, and order and discipline once more became the order of the day.

Rumours soon came creeping through the lines of a change in the leadership of the enemy's forces, but as yet they lay quietly within the city and showed not the teeth of offence. Thus we lay on the green hillsides of Valley Forge, busily preparing for the struggle which was certain to come, until far into the spring, without a sign of a movement on the part of the enemy.

But with May came their new Commander-in-Chief, Sir Henry Clinton, and the departure of Lord Howe, and we knew that the time had at last come when some bold stroke would be played in the game of war.

The gaps in our ranks had been somewhat filled, and we were ready and eager for active service as soon as the great General would give the command.

At last came rumours of a retreat, that the English were preparing to desert the city and march across the plains of Jersey to where New York lay, sheltered by the waters of the sea and the rivers. We marched toward the Delaware to be ready to strike them when they moved.

So, one day, as I stood on the outpost, guarding the nearest road to the city, I saw Jones approaching at full speed on an old horse, which he had evidently borrowed. I was ready for his news.

"The British are crossing the Delaware; we will catch them in Jersey now or never," he cried, and then he had dashed past on his way to headquarters.

My little guard received the news with a yell, and we looked forward eagerly for the order to join our regiment on the march.

It was not long in coming, and on that night, the 18th of June, we crossed the Delaware, and started on the race across Jersey that was to end at Monmouth.

CHAPTER XIX

THE SANDS OF MONMOUTH

For a week we hung on the flank of the enemy, waiting for an opportunity to strike, as we saw the immense train form on the right bank of the Delaware and take up its cumbersome march across the Jersey plains.

With it marched the whole force of the British army of seventeen thousand men, who did their duty so well that we longed for an opening in vain.

All through those blazing hot days of June we marched through the sands of Jersey, ankle deep as we trudged along, and it seemed as if the time for a trial of strength would never come. All to the east and south of us the great train of their wagons crawled along through the heat and the dust, and the sun glinted and gleamed on the points of the bayonets as the mass of their troops marched on.

Slowly they crawled through the dusty roads of Jersey, and slowly they were crawling beyond the reach of our arms into the haven of safety.

At last, on the 27th of the month, they reached the heights of Monmouth, within a day's march of their journey's end, while we lay five miles away at Englishtown, swearing low and earnestly at our luck.

That night there came news to the camp that put new life in the men, and made them forget the heat and the toil of the march; the news that the great General had decided to risk a throw in the morning, and that our regiment was to be with the advance.

And so, when Lee rode up to take command, we gave him a cheer, for though we disliked and distrusted the man, yet his coming meant a fight in the morning.

Then there was a great stir in the camp; the men saw to their muskets, and the signs everywhere told of their eager preparations for the deadly struggle in the morning, while the cheery laugh and the snatches of song spoke well for the spirits of the men after the long, toilsome march of the day.

The sun comes up out of the ocean early in Jersey, but even before its rays had cleared the pine tops our camp was stirring with life, the men preparing for the advance.

But there seemed to be a fatality about it all; a hand, as it were, covered us and held us back, paralyzing the spirit of the men.

Delay followed delay, and when at last the regiments took up the line of march, ours was held back until almost the last. The New Jersey volunteers had the post of honour, as they longed to revenge their ruined homesteads and devastated farms, and then our turn came.

We marched out of Englishtown into the dreary country beyond. On every side sand dunes, former barriers of the ocean, raised their crests, covered with a straggling forest of stunted pines and scrub trees, which, in the passes in the hills, came down to the road, disputing the passageway, while in the shallow valleys lay the open fields and marshes. A dreary country withal, but where a small body of troops could hold the passes in the hills against many hundreds and make good their defence.

We passed through the defile in the first range of hills, crossed the low valley, and then, after passing through the second defile, we had only to cross the one before us to be on the heights overlooking the enemy's position at Freehold.

As we approached this last pass in the hills we were surprised to see a steady stream of our troops coming back in disorder through the gap. The men were retreating doggedly in broken ranks, and turning, as they trudged along, to look back, as if with half a mind to return.

As they came streaming past our advance I called to a sergeant, an old backwoodsman whose courage I knew, and asked him of the battle and why he was not fighting.

"Fight?" he cried indignantly, "why, damn it, Lieutenant, they will not let us fight. They ordered us to retreat before a musket was fired."

At that moment Captain Mercer, an aide of the staff of General Lee, rode up to Colonel Ramsay, who was near me.

He delivered an order rapidly, and then I heard Ramsay's voice ring out angrily. "Retreat?" he cried. "By whose order?"

"By the order of General Lee."

"But," he protested hotly, "we have not seen the enemy yet."

Mercer shrugged his shoulders. "I only carry the order," he said.

The stream of fugitives grew rapidly, becoming more disorderly, showing at every step the spread of the panic and the rout, as Colonel Ramsay stopped the advance and gave the order to retreat.

Slowly and reluctantly we obeyed, and as we retired through the second pass in the hills we saw the British gain the opposite ridge and advance with cheers on the disorderly flying mass in the sandy valley behind.

Every moment the press of the fugitives grew greater, and though we still maintained our formation and marched as on parade the retreat had turned into a rout. On every side and in our rear the broken ranks of the army poured past, demoralised and in despair, and ever nearer came the musketry and the cheers of the advancing English.

"They will catch us before we get through the gap," said Dick, looking at the pass in front of us.

"Then we will fight anyhow," I replied, "and General Lee can go to the devil."

Whereupon our spirits began to pick up, and the men retreated more slowly than ever, glancing over their shoulders to see how near the head of the British column was.

At last we came to the foot of the first pass, with its hills heavily covered with scrub pines. Behind us stretched the fields of broken troops, and we could see the red line of the British as they debouched upon the plain and drove the patriots before them.

It was a wild scene of confusion and disorder, of demoralised retreat and rout; and then something happened.

There was a stir in the pass in our front, a clatter of hoofs, and there appeared before us the General with his staff. He towered there with his great figure, a veritable god of war and of wrath.

For a moment his eye swept the field, and his face flushed crimson with indignation and anger, as he saw the best troops of his army flying like sheep before the enemy. There was a storm in the air, and then, as Lee rode up, it broke.

We heard his excited "Sir, sir!" and the General's angry tones, and then dismissing him contemptuously, he called to Hamilton to ask if there was a regiment which could stop the advance.

Ramsay sprang forward.

"My regiment is ready, General."

"If you stop them ten minutes until I form, you will save the army."

"I will stop them or fall," cried Ramsay, and, turning to us, he gave the order to "About face," and then crying that the General relied on us to save the army, he led us in the charge.

Not a moment too soon, for, as the press of the fugitives was brushed aside by our advance, mingling in the midst of the disorderly mass, came the red line of the British, cheering and victorious.

But suddenly the flying mass disappeared, and in their place came the yell of the Maryland Line, the long array of their bayonets bent to the charge, with all the fury and weight of their onset.

For a moment the red line hesitated; then an officer, who looked strangely familiar, sprang forward, shouting:

"They are nothing but dogs of rebels; charge and break them."

The red line answered with a cheer, for their fighting blood was up, and they dashed forward to meet us.

Then came such a clash of steel as is seldom heard, as the King's Grenadiers and the Maryland Line met in the shock of the charge. For a moment so close was the press that we could not wield our arms, and men fell, spitted on each other's bayonets.

Then came a deadly struggle, as men fought desperately, hand to hand, and the lines swayed backward and forward as the weight of the numbers told. The ground was lost and gained, struggled for and won over and over, while the dead lay in heaps under our feet.

It was in the midst of this deadly struggle, when I was fighting sword in hand amid the press of bayonets for my very life, that I saw Ramsay, who was near, cheering on his men, come face to face with the officer who led the charge of the Grenadiers. Then, in that storm centre, around which the roar of battle raged, there was a flash of steel and the swords crossed. But in the fury of the battle duels are short and fierce, and I saw Ramsay, who was already covered with wounds, falter for a moment, as the other lunged, and then he was down among the slain.

Our line hesitated as Ramsay fell, and the English pressed on with a cheer. But I sprang forward, shouting to the men to save their Colonel, and they, answering my call, forced the English back, until I stood by Ramsay's body. But only for a moment; before we could raise Ramsay gently up and bear him off the field, there came another charge of the Grenadiers that forced us off our feet and hurled us backward, fighting desperately, leaving the body of our Colonel in the hands of the enemy. But in the *mêlée* I found my sword crossing that of the officer who had fought with Ramsay, and instantly I attacked him fiercely, for I was burning to avenge Ramsay's fall. But he, with ease and coolness, parried all my thrusts and played with me as if I were but a child. Then, as I was growing desperate, he called to me, "Nay, lad, go try your sword on some one else and leave an old Scot alone. I would not hurt you for the world."

I started and let the point of my sword fall, for it was the voice of the old Tory, whom I had not before recognised in the confusion of the fight. This slight hesitation almost led to my capture, for I had been fighting in advance of our line, and now I found myself in the midst of the English troops. So, saluting the old Tory hastily, I regained our lines.

Then, fighting foot by foot and inch, by inch, we contested their advance, as the weight of numbers bore us backward up the hill into the pines. But every minute gained meant the salvation of the army.

Ah, it was hot work there, ankle deep in the sand, with the broiling sun above us, while the smoke and the dust of the conflict filled our throats and eyes; but we staggered on and fought blindly, desperately, amid the din and the carnage.

Ten minutes, twenty minutes—ah, there it is at last, and the roar of the opening battle broke out to the right and left of us, as the re-formed regiments went into the fight.

Then to our left came the high piercing yell of our brothers of the Line, and we knew that the British were falling back before them. The Grenadiers struggled on for a moment longer, but the force of their charge was spent, and the fire of the new regiments forced them back in turn.

But it was only for awhile, for they re-formed, and, under the leadership of the gallant Monkton, hurled themselves upon us once again.

Monkton fell, and their lines shrivelled up under our fire. Then, as it was near the setting of the sun, Washington, glancing over the field, saw that the time had come and ordered the advance.

Our whole line sprang forward, and, though we had borne the brunt, the toil, and heat of the day, not a man faltered. As the long line swept forward the British slowly retreated before us. We drove them across the plain and through the second pass, where night overtook us and stopped our pursuit.

But then, when the fever of the battle left us, a great fatigue seized hold of our limbs, the men sank to the earth as they stood, and slept from very exhaustion.

But we were soon to be aroused.

Through the darkness came the sound of a horse's hoofs, and a voice, asking for Ramsay's regiment. I sprang up, answering, and saw approaching a body of horsemen. The foremost rider seemed an immense figure, as he advanced in the darkness; but I, who had seen him often before, knew him to be the great General.

I immediately gave the alarm, and the men sprang to their feet and presented arms.

And then, there under the pines, by the light of the stars, the General rode down our line, and, coming to the centre, we felt his glance fall over our ranks.

"Men of Maryland," spoke Washington, and his voice rang clear through the pines, "once before at Long Island you saved the army, and today, for a second time, you have done so by your courage and tenacity. I thank you in the name of the army and the nation; I thank you for myself."

A wild yell that broke from the Line was his answer. We forgot our fatigue and our wounds in the pride of the moment.

CHAPTER XX

IN THE LINES OF THE ENEMY

It was near the end of the first watch when an order came to me to pick out several men, go forward, feel the enemy's outposts, and see if the enemy was still retreating.

Making my choice, I passed our pickets with three men, and made my way cautiously to the last pass in the hills which was in the enemy's possession at nightfall. But not a sign of their pickets or troops could I find; so I boldly advanced in the pass, and, crossing the ridge, found myself on the heights overlooking Freehold. It was a small town of scattered houses, and beyond it I could see the lights of the British camp-fires.

But as the heights were not near enough for our purpose, we descended into the plain, and carefully made our way toward the town, where I knew certain patriots were, who, if I could once get speech with them, would tell me the whole plans of the enemy.

We could hear the tramp of feet at the further side of the village, and all the sounds of an army in retreat. Being now so close to them, and in great danger, we moved with the utmost caution. Near at hand, on the outskirts of the town, stood a large, square stone house, separated from the rest of the houses by an immense garden. Having found a break in the hedge, we entered.

It was an old garden, filled with boxwood walks and flowers run wild. Very prim at one time it must have been; but, now that the war had helped the return to nature, it was a wild and tangled mass.

Making our way through the garden, a light was suddenly thrown upon our path, and, glancing up, I saw that it came from a window which, though it was on the first floor of the house, was yet some distance from the ground.

Then the figure of a woman crossed the window, stopping for a moment to look out, while we stood in the shadow of the hedge, holding our breath. But she passed on, and I, determining to see into the room to discover whether it contained friend or foe, quickly gained the shelter of the wall of the house. The wall was of rough hewn stone, and with the help of my comrades' shoulders, I raised myself high enough to glance over the window-sill, and what I saw there made me drop to the ground quickly.

Then, whispering to my comrades to stay where they were, I made my way to the rear entrance of the house, and, finding the door unfastened, softly entered the hall; and then I was standing in the door of the room from which the light came.

A lamp stood on a table near a long horse-hair sofa with spindle legs, on which lay the figure of a man. The coat had been cut from his shoulder, which was swathed in many bandages, while the blood-stained rags on the table and the floor told of the seriousness of the wound.

A slender figure was bending over him, gently arranging a pillow under his head.

"Do you feel easier now, father?"

"Yes, lassie." Then, a moment later, "Why does not Clinton send me a carriage? He surely does not intend to desert me here."

"Captain Farquharson is searching for one," she answered. And then turning to the table, she saw me standing in the doorway. The colour left her face; she gave a little cry, for she thought there were many men behind me, and that all was lost. So, quickly putting my finger to my lips, I stepped back into the darkness of the hall, and as I did so, I heard the old Tory ask, "What's that?"

"It was nothing," she answered. "I thought I saw a ghost."

I stood there in the broad window waiting, for I knew she would come.

Below me was the garden, heavy-scented with the odour of flowers, and the hum of the night insects was everywhere in the air. Close to the wall I saw the figures of my scouts. The noise of the tramp of feet, the creak of waggons, and the voice of command came to me from the village street.

At last she came and stood before me. In her eyes were great pain and fear and suffering.

"Tell me," she asked anxiously, "is there any danger for him?"

"More danger for me than for him," I replied. "The whole American advance guard consists of three men and myself; the rest will follow in the morning."

"Ah," she cried, and there was hope once more in her voice; "then we can escape."

"If you can move your father by sunrise, yes," I replied.

"But you," she said, and there was new anxiety in her voice; "you are in great danger here. When the soldiers come to remove father they will take you prisoner."

"I care not, Mistress Jean," I answered, "for your eyes have held me prisoner for many a long day, and all the prison bars in the world are nothing to me so long as I can look into them."

"Nay," she said, "you must not say such things to me."

And I, taking this as a confirmation of all my fears and that at last Farquharson had succeeded in his suit, would have bade her good-bye and gone my way. But before I went I told her of my wishes for her happiness, and that I had met Farquharson and knew of his skill and courage.

"Farquharson?" and her eyes were wide open in surprise. "I really believe you think I am going to marry him;" and she laughed so softly, bewitchingly, that—

"Jean, Jean," I cried, now that hope and life had come back with a rush, "Jean, do you know that I love you; that I love the very ground on which you walk, the sunbeams in your hair, the very air you breathe? Ah! Jean—" But at that moment came the voice of the Tory calling her and the tramp of feet on the porch.

"Let me go," she cried, for I held her hands in mine; "and fly,—that is the guard."

"Nay," said I, "not till you give me a kiss. I will stay here and be captured first."

There was a moment's hesitation, and then a flash of white arms, and the softest caress—ah, such a caress that the memory of it will go with me to the grave. And then she was gone.

And I, not wishing to be captured now, slipped through the rear door to my men, and a short time later, having satisfied ourselves of the retreat of the enemy's forces, we made our way back over the hills to report to the General.

We followed the enemy closely the next day, and did not draw off until we saw them beyond our reach at Sandy Hook.

Then we took our way to the Jersey hills, and lay there for a time watching the enemy in New York.

CHAPTER XXI

THE PASSING OF YEARS

Then came a long period when it seemed almost as if peace had settled over the land, so seldom did the rattle of musket fire or the angry flash of guns break the quiet repose of the Jersey plains and farms.

Far across the marshes lay New York, and behind its walls and the broad sweep of the waters the British army rested safe, while the army of the patriots, scattered among the forests, woods, and hills of Jersey and New York, lived, like Robin Hood's followers of old, and waited while the wheel of fortune turned.

A year went by, when at the taking of Paulus Hook I first heard news of the welfare of the Tory and the maid, since the night of the Monmouth retreat.

It was after an all-night march through the marshes of Jersey, often breast-high in the water, that we made a silent, deadly charge with the bayonet on the enemy's fort, and carried it before the sun had risen.

We were retiring rapidly, after securing our prisoners, when one of my men called to me: "Captain, here's one of those Highland chiefs knocked on the head."

I went to him and found that it was Farquharson, who had received an ugly blow on the head from a clubbed musket.

A little whiskey between his teeth and water on his face revived him, and I was able, with the help of several men, to carry him along with our party.

We made good our retreat, and when several days later I was in the main camp of the army, I went to the quarters where the prisoners were detained, and there I again met Farquharson.

"Captain," said he, smiling, for he had almost recovered from his wound, "there is no entering a contest against you; fortune is always on your side."

"My turn will come," I answered; "but is there anything I can do for you?"

"I am afraid not, unless you bribe the guards to let me escape."

"That would be clear against the articles of war," I replied. We fell to talking, and then it was I heard of the Tory and his daughter.

"It was about Christmas time," said Farquharson, "that the King sent a message over the sea, granting him a pardon for the part he had taken in '45, for you know he was out then. The Sea

Raven was about to clear in a week for Glasgow, and a sudden longing seemed to seize him to see once more the dash of the waters through the Braes of Mar and the heather-crowned hills of old Aberdeen; and so, within a week, they had sailed away; and as he left he said to me: 'A revolt drove me from old Scotland; another sends me back again. I wonder where fortune will end my days.' It is a strange fortune that has followed him through life."

"It is, indeed," I replied.

So they sailed away over the seas, gone back to their own land and people; and between that land and mine burned high the flame of war. But through the flame and across the broad stretch of the waters, I saw the form of the maid beckoning me on, and though my hope was well-nigh gone, I buckled tight my sword-belt and doggedly went on,—went on, through the long march to the southward, the toil, the hunger, and the defeat of the Camden campaign.

The great triumph of Eutaw Springs and Cowpens, as we drove back Cornwallis from the hill country to the shore, rolled back the tide of invasion and drowned it in the sea.

A year went by, bringing me adventures not a few, and with the adventures came wounds and honours; and when there came the news of the leaguer of Yorktown, it found me a full Colonel in the army of the South.

It was not my fortune to be present at that last great feat of our arms, when the great General struck the blow that freed us for ever from the tyranny of the King.

But when the news came down to us in the savannahs of the South we hailed it with joy, for we saw once more before us the quiet, smiling fields of Maryland, with the ease and comfort and plenty of it all that awaited but our coming to repay us for the years of strife and blood.

And then at last came the order for us to take up the homeward march. The men took up the trail with as jaunty a step as when they first marched to the northward, long years before. The gay uniforms were faded and gone; rags and tatters had taken their places, while of the brave banner that was flung to the breeze at the Head of Elk nothing remained but the staff and a few ribbons that flaunted therefrom.

But every tatter told the tale of a fight where the shot and shell had torn it as it waved above the charging line, the deadly struggle of the hand to hand, or marked the slow and sullen retreat.

The men themselves were hardy and bronzed; from their ragged caps to their soleless shoes they bore the stamp of veterans.

They showed the signs of their training in the angry school of war; wide indeed was the difference between the gay volunteers of '76 and the hardy veterans of '82. We swung along in our homeward march with a right goodwill, and at last came to the broad Potomac and saw the hills of Maryland beyond.

Now the river itself to the low water-line of the southern bank is within the boundaries of Maryland. Wishing to be the first across the line, I rode my horse in to the saddle-girths, and let him drink thereof.

A day later brought us to Annapolis, where we received the thanks of the State authorities, and with all due form and ceremony obtained our discharge and then dispersed to our homes.

That very day I took a canoe, and, crossing the bay, found myself again on the steps of Fairlee.

Once more my mother leaned on my arm, and, looking up at her tall, broad-shouldered son, with his epaulets of a Colonel, bronzed face, and hardy bearing, seemed proud and happy.

CHAPTER XXII

THE COMING OF THE MAID

Many months had passed away, spring had come again, and the fair city of Annapolis lay in a mass of flowers. The vivid green of the old trees cast a delightful shade over all, tempting one to stroll through the quiet streets and byways, past the moss-grown walls, the old-fashioned gardens, buried in roses, and the stately, proud mansions of many of Maryland's best and bravest.

I was standing on a step and above me stood Mistresses Polly and Betsy Johnson, who were railing at me now that I no longer wore a uniform and was simply a plain member of the Legislature.

"He looked so fine in his brass buttons," said Mistress Polly.

"A brave, bold, quite proper-looking young fellow," added Mistress Betsy.

"And now just look at him," continued Mistress Polly pathetically; and they surveyed me sorrowfully, while malicious mischief played around the corners of their eyes.

I laughed outright. I could not help it, so droll was the expression on their faces.

"True, your ladyship," I said; "the toga does not fit a young man so well as the buckled sabre and glittering epaulets. But now that dull peace has come, the hall of the Legislature is the only place where you can throw the weight of your sword in the conflict and wield some influence in the great struggles of the country; would you have me idle?"

"Nay, I would not have that," said Mistress Polly judiciously. "But your round head and big hands are just the things for a fight, and though your voice is—well—can be heard a considerable distance, I am afraid——" She paused, as if doubtful about its being put to any good use in the hall of the Assembly.

Decidedly I was getting the worst of it.

At this moment Dick Ringgold, who represented Kent with me, came swinging up the street, and, seeing me standing on the steps, hailed me with—

"Hello, Frisby, have you heard the news?"

"What news?"

"Your old Tory friend Gordon is on the Sally Ann, from London, which has just come up the harbour."

"Any one with him?" I asked anxiously.

"Well," said Dick, maliciously drawling it out, "I heard some one say there was a young lady with him."

I did not stop to protest against the laughter that followed me as I dashed down the street, or to Dick's shout as he called something after me. A few minutes later I was on the wharf.

Out in the stream, swaying with the current of the tide, lay the Sally Ann, her tall spars tapering high in air, her decks full of bustle and activity, showing the journey's end and that the final preparations for disembarkation were under full headway.

As I arrived a boat was pulling off from her side containing two passengers. As I saw them my heart gave a great bound; my hand went to my hat and swung it around my head. In answer to my signal came the fluttering of a handkerchief.

"Sir," said I, as the old Tory stepped ashore, "let me be the first to welcome you back to old Maryland."

"Would that all my enemies were like you!" he replied. "I hesitated long about returning, but Jean would have it so."

And Mistress Jean said not a word as I took her hand in mine, but her face was mantled in scarlet and her eyes were downcast.

The prim old garden of the Nicholsons never looked more charming, the flowers more sweet and beautiful, or the green boxwood hedges more suggestive of rest and repose; the lazy waters of the Chester rolled along at its foot, gently lapping the grass. Ah! the sun was shining on a glorious world that day, for Mistress Jean walked beside me.

"Mistress Jean," said I, as we stood where the waters met the grass and looked out over the broad and silent river, flowing on and on as if to eternity, "our lives have been more like mountain torrents than the broad smooth river here. We have lived through the battles and sieges, seen blood and death and all the horrors of a great war, but now that peace has come, and our course lies through pleasant fields and verdant meadows, would it not be best for them to join and flow on as this great river does, Jean? Ah, Jean, you know how much I love you."

And then she placed her hand in mine; her eyes spoke that which I most wished to know, and the very earth seemed glorious.

I know not how long we stood there, when there came Mistress Nancy Nicholson's voice through the garden, calling, "Jean, Jean, where are you?"

"Here," she answered; and with that Mistress Nancy came running round the hedge.

"Oh, Jean," she cried, "Dick has proposed."

And then, seeing me, she stamped her little foot, and cried, "Oh, bother!" blushing meanwhile as red as one of her roses.

"And so have I, Mistress Nancy," I replied.

And now, my children, I end this tale, sitting here on the old porch at Fairlee. The pen drops from my hand, but my eyes are not too dim to see the flash of the sunlight on the waters of the great bay through the break in the trees.

Nor are they too dim, Miss Jean, in spite of the impertinent toss of your head, to see in you the likeness of the maid that led me such a wild dance in the days of my youth. And I promise you, if you do not smile on young Dick Ringgold and stop your outrageous treatment of him, I will not leave you a cent in my will.

There, there; I retract every word that I said. Was there ever so audacious a monkey in the world?

There, I have finished. Oh, yes, I forgot—

"John Cotton, bring me some more mint."

THE END